C

MW01536947

WARNING:

¡Advertencia!

The following record of the first epic part of Rigby Cross's life is explained in the following. Read at your own risk. Danger, suspense, and funny happenings may occur. If any symptoms of diarrhea, uncontrollable giggles, pants-peeing, loss of breath, or any other catastrophic occurrences ensue, the recorder may not be responsible. Parental discretion may or may not be advised.

To my fam, and dormant artists

1

Mrs. Sleepyhead

St. Anne's Place was an unprecedented middle school that lay a few miles from the coast of California. It was a few decades old, but was in great condition. Its dark, brown, smoothed clay covered the wood and steel that kept the building up. Gothic caramel brown ridges lay below the windows and above grand doors, with intricate engravings of angels.

The classrooms were fairly big, even though there were thirty kids in a classroom, each spaced apart a yard or so.

The whole school sat on ten acres, most of which were utilized by religious related structures like churches, school buildings, and a Sisters' Convent. About three or so acres were used for play areas and parking space.

You could say the school rooms looked like a medieval church, which yes, partially were true since it was a Catholic school, and gothic architecture seem to entangle itself with Catholicism in the Middle Ages.

It had a church of the same design, except it was much grander, pointier, and more artistic than the already fabulous school itself. Some called it "The Medieval Mission," because it wasn't too far from the location of other missions.

However, its exterior wasn't the reason why it was so well known. The altar was the most elegant and stunning piece of the whole school.

A replica of Jesus on the Cross was literally *floating*. That was if you let your eyes play tricks on you. It was actually hung up by thin, clear cables that allowed the Cross to appear suspended in midair, acknowledging the power of Jesus.

In front of it, a long marble arch separated the altar's boundaries. The stairs were marble too, and the Presider's chair was cushioned with brown leather that matched the outside of the Church.

The school was taught by nuns who happily kept order, and enjoyed cracking down on teen boys who couldn't keep their mouths shut when they were supposed to about certain topics.

It was the nuns, after all, who kept the record for Highest Grade-Scoring Catholic School award seven years in a row. They taught all classes except for seventh grade. Seventh grade was an interesting place because of that. Mrs. Cornhusker was the seventh-grade teacher, and she hated failure and messes. Many of her failing and messy students would always try to sing or bore her to sleep because of her utterly boring way of teaching. Many different methods were tried, and immunobiology and corn shucking among the most successful topics that would put her to sleep.

Though an abundant number of ideas and thoughts were brought for experiment; only a blank stare from Mrs. Cornhusker would come closest to success.

On the first day of school, it was business as usual and they all attempted to get Mrs. Cornhusker to sleep. But yet again to their disappointment, not a single seventh grader was successful—except for the new kid. That new kid had no idea about "Mrs. Cornhusker sleeping attempts." Right? That's what Rigby Cross thought.

That *new* kid, Francis, went on a long lecture about sanitation and pathogens trying to get out of doing work. Once the teacher fell asleep, it was utter destruction around the class. The girls gossiped while the boys threw paper airplanes that barely flew a few feet. Rigby wondered if the teacher would wake up ready to bark nonsense instructions for peace in her blank mind. He also wondered if he'd be the first one to blow up the classroom. There had to be vinegar and baking soda somewhere…

Rigby was a regular dude who enjoyed the company of people. His brown hair was long enough for some school administrator to tell him to cut it, but it wasn't that noticeable. His friends didn't care bout his hair cut, it didn't hurt anyone—but was it being disrespectful? Well, maybe, but that depended on who you asked.

He had it combed to the right side of his head and made sure not to put too much hair product on.

His uniform consisted of a light blue collared shirt, navy pants, and a smile which could make girls weep for more. On special occasions, he wears his Lucky Undies. He had no idea how this superstitious idea crossed his mind, but it appeared to work. His green and denim striped underwear were lucky indeed. He had as much popularity as a seventh grade, handsome, all around awesome, honest, and extraverted guy could have at St. Anne's Place.

So when this new wimpy kid who looked a whole year younger than him, made Mrs. Cornhusker go "night night" Rigby was dumbfounded. He lost all attention from his fellow classmates, while they veered toward Francis. He was jealous no doubt, and he figured he shouldn't expect "You're so Cute!" cards five times a day anymore from the girls.

Those cards were pretty legit too. Rigby could tell they spent a whole afternoon on them.

He hoped they didn't get too hopped up on Francis's new popularity, because he'd really miss denying an early engagement. Not that he *had* a girlfriend. In fact, he found that idea quite ludicrous because it was hard for him to get attached to people.

Once lunch recess began, he made sure to walk up to Francis before his former throng of followers adored his sleep-mesmerizing abilities. As soon as the bell rang, he snuck past the lag of people in his way. Mrs. Cornhusker finally woke up, but she was out of line to instruct them before recess.

He had guessed that Francis already beat everyone out the door first, and was correct. Rigby waded his way through the other grades and spotted Francis a few yards away.

Francis wore the same uniform as Rigby, but his brownish-orangish hair was curly and slightly untidy.

Rigby crept up behind a bench, and said, "Uh, hey. Nice job on your sleep magic."

Francis jumped. "Oh—! Oh, uh, hi." he said, startled.

Rigby stepped back a little bit. "Sorry, I didn't mean to—"

Francis sighed nervously. "Yeah, it's okay. I have a phobia of not knowing enough."

Rigby nodded. He could partially agree. If you were the head classmate, you had to know a lot. But mostly knowing how to pretend you knew a lot was better. Kind of like a politician with lots of advisors.

6

He put his hands in his pockets.

"So, good job on putting Mrs. Cornhusker to sleep."

Francis frowned. "Uh, I didn't try to do that."

Now Rigby frowned. "You didn't try to do that?"

"No, actually. I did that on accident. I have another phobia. I'm an A100 germaphobe."

Rigby just stood there confused. He had never been this confused before in his life. "What's an A100 germaphobe?" he asked.

"It's the topmost level of germaphobia. I don't know how reliable that is, considering I learned that from a 'dot net' website that wanted to use cookies, so for all I know, it could be inconclusive."

Rigby smiled. "Spoken like a scientist."

Francis frowned again. "Um, why do you say that?"

"Because you put Mrs. Cornhusker to sleep with science."

"That's all?"

"Nah, I don't know what inconclusive means." Rigby admitted.

Francis gave a slight laugh. "Get that a lot."

Then Rigby had a random idea. An idea so great, it could change his life. He could get his popularity back! "Um, Francis?"

7

"Hmm?" Francis responded.

"Do you want to go to the spice shop right by the beach?"

"Why," he asked confused, "is there a spice shop? How does that survive?"

Rigby shrugged. "Why do goats have four stomachs? Is having four stomachs the key to being the greatest of all time?"

"Okay," Francis said. "I'll go. But four stomachs aren't the key. I think cattle have four stomachs too."

"Whatever. I want to talk about a few things." Rigby continued. "Y'know, like if you wanted to be my unofficial sidekick kind-of-thing. And if you wanted the right kind of attention."

Francis frowned. "Why should I be concerned about the right kind of attention? This is a decent school, right? At my last school, I learned something I shouldn't every day."

Rigby knew that was coming and chuckled. "Well, those peeps over there," Rigby pointed a hundred feet away from him toward the seventh graders, "are the bad kind of attention. I got a nasty bruise on the right side of my jaw." Rigby lied.

Francis looked a little concerned now.

"No, no, no," Rigby said nonchalantly, "They're good friends actually. You just have to learn how to *control* them through wits and the power of

8

persuasion. I learned from class one day that today's modern technology has made modern society like sheep. You have to be the shepherd."

Rigby had to say persuasion slowly so he wouldn't mess it up and sound kind of dumb in front of a person way smarter.

Francis nodded quickly, seeing they were getting closer. "I don't do well in crowds either," Francis added hastily. "I—I'll see you there after school."

Rigby smiled. "Good choice bro. See ya!" and he walked away from the crowd coming toward Francis. The crowd was praising him.

Good, Rigby thought. *I guess I'll obtain my crowd again sooner than I thought. Once in the spice shop, I'll just tell him the popular guy is with me, and then I'll just let my instincts take over. Once the crowd is back under my control, I'll dump him like an old sack of potatoes heading for the garbage can.*

He smiled once more and set off for a basketball hoop. *I love those Lucky Undies.*

2

Behind the Door

Rigby was waiting for Francis. Normally, he would purposefully enter meetings late, but he figured he should at least be *five* minutes late, respectively. Once he arrived, he thought Francis would be there waiting, but no. *He* was late now.

He swore he saw Francis multiple times when kids went to the Employees only door and didn't return. They were chatting in low whispers, concealing excitement.

After school, he reminded Francis once more about his appointment. He said he had to complete at least one assignment first, and then he'd walk down to the shop. Apparently, that one subject took two hours, because he arrived when Rigby was about to give up, walk out, and go home.

Francis came into sight.

"Sorry I wasn't precise with the time." he apologized.

Rigby shrugged. "No worries, bro. Though I admit, I thought you forgot."

Francis made a nervous laugh.

"Well, I'm not allowed to go on my own yet. My family and I just moved to the coast here in

California, and they need to know the surrounding place better. Well, my parents do at least. I memorized a map of here in Pismo. I had to finish all my homework, triple check, and sneak out."

Rigby nodded. "So, anyways," he said in a business-like voice, "You want to know how to be with the right crowd?"

"Yep." Francis responded.

"Well, there's only one rule."

"Really?" Francis asked. Rigby nodded again.

"One rule?" Francis clarified. Rigby nodded a little taken back. How many times does this kid have to check?

"What's the rule then?" Francis said.

"Stick with me and watch and learn." Rigby responded.

Francis frowned. "Three steps, then?"

Rigby held back some anger. "Whatever. Three steps then."

Francis nodded his head.

"When do I start?"

"Whenever you like. Tomorrow might be best. You can get a head start. All you have to do is watch and learn, really."

Francis nodded. He appeared to think that this wasn't a good idea, noting his look of skepticism.

Seeing this, Rigby added, "Want a little pre-practice? It seems irrelevant to the current situation at hand, but the idea is the same."

"Sure."

Rigby gestured toward Francis to follow him. He followed him until Rigby reached the Employees Only door. "Ready?" he asked.

"For what?" Francis said. Rigby frowned. "To see what's behind this door."

Francis stepped back. "No chance."

Rigby started to feel his anger slip. "You said you wanted help. Right?"

"Yeah, but I don't want to do something illegal!"

"Do you really think this is illegal!?"

"Yeah! It says employees only!"

"Well, to me, it says 'Come and see what's inside!'"

"Looks like you need to go back to Kindergar—

Rigby ignored him and grabbed him by his shirt collar and dragged him inside.

Typically, you would see a mini factory made for making cinnamon rolls. Today, you would look and find yourself in a tree trunk with four holes surrounding you.

"What the—" Rigby clamped Francis's mouth shut. They just stood there like that for a few moments in silence, until Rigby broke it. "THIS IS AWESOME!"

Francis jumped.

Rigby started running happily out of the tree trunk. On each side, there was a hole that showed a two-lane road.

"C'mon, Francis! Let's explore!" Rigby forgot their argument, and Francis looked scared, but he listened.

Rigby had never felt more alive before. Controlling a group of people, who cared! Adventure awaited him! Francis's mood seemed as if it tried to dampen it, but he continued to set it alight with every new thing he saw. Out of the tree, he saw a whole city. On the left, he saw buildings with people calling out and making deals, exchanging money and items. On the right, he saw a grand honey colored church behind a delicate fountain gushing water from a man pouring out water from a conch. It was John the Baptist.

Behind the church, he caught a glimpse of grapevines and a small wheat field.

He turned around running, Francis struggling to catch up.

On his left, larger buildings stood before him. These ones smelled of food, and strangely, guacamole. Immediately, he felt hungry and his stomach rumbled. The scent of food seemed to be coming from a store called "Cornerstone Bakery" and "Holy Molly's Guacamole." He decided he would get some bagels topped with guacamole later if he could.

On his right, a large building almost as high as the sky loomed over them. It held colorful banners and was made of cobblestone. Its top had dark brown tiles covering pointed domes. Once Francis had caught up, he gazed up too in awe. Rigby would've probably looked more, but someone shouted to Francis and him.

"Hello! Hel-l-o-o! Uh, boys! Ugh, I will regret saying this. Bros!"

Rigby and Francis shook their heads and snapped back to reality at the word "bros."

Rigby had to make sure what he was looking at when he looked that direction. No way.

It was a girl. But not just any girl. She was maybe a little older than Rigby (to his disappointment) but he didn't realize he was staring at her, until Francis slapped him in the face and smiled apologetically at her.

The girl frowned. "Have you been here before?" she asked slightly annoyed.

"Nope." Francis had to do the talking, because Rigby couldn't quite pull himself together. Rigby could tell Francis was still struggling with shock from their strange appearance in a tree.

"Did you, um, see people come through the employees only door?" she said stealing a glance from Rigby, looking slightly worried and confused, but amused in a way.

"Yeah, um, Rigby here deliberately pulled me into the door. Why?"

She shrugged. "Seven people new about each year come here without a reason, do the same thing you do, usually. I'm Marie."

She said "usually" at Rigby, frowning.

Rigby couldn't remember much after that, but once he was out of his love trance ten minutes later, he realized Francis was guiding him up the stairs of the big cobblestone building. He just noticed there were large outdoor sports arenas too.

"W—what was her name?" Rigby asked Francis. Francis laughed a little. "Snap back to reality again, Loveboy?" Rigby shook his head. They propped themselves up against the stairs of the cobblestone building.

"What was her name?" Rigby asked again.

"I don't know. You should've asked." Francis lied, not wanting to touch the subject.

Rigby fumed. "Dang it." he said under his breath.

"Plus," Francis said, "she's probably like, three years older than you, and way taller." Rigby shrugged, extremely depressed.

"Anyways," Francis said awkwardly, "this talk is getting extremely uncomfortable."

Francis told Rigby why they were here in a new place. It was called Hadash Eden, which was "New Eden" in Hebrew.

Apparently, seven kids between ages eleven and twelve somehow get through the employees only door every year around this time in January. They have to attend a school called Hadash Eden Basafel, or HEB, somehow, because the seven were "destined" to. Francis substituted "destined" for "supposed to, and would end up there sooner or later."

The school was the grand cobblestone building. It was essentially your regular school, aside from learning how to slay dragons and demons with real weapons, blowing stuff up with vials of potions and poisons, and making some super cool inventions with craftsmanship. Rigby liked the dragon part, while Francis liked the chemistry part.

There were four periods of time each grade, usually between one to two years. Their first year, they would be called starters. The next period would be learners, then apprentices, then graduals.

The start of the term would be on January first, tomorrow, and would end November twentieth the next year. There were no breaks to go home because the intermediate dimension between this city and the Earth were closed.

They were given assignments throughout the term. They could stay at a motel catered for students in Hadash Eden for a nightly cost, or they could stay at the school dorms. The school dorms were in the school building, a few for the boys and a few for the girls. It was most common to be in the motel, because there wasn't much room in the dorms.

End of term assignments were due until November twentieth of next year.

Marie had quickly gone over it, giving them tips on how to get the items they needed for the term. They'd have to swing by a couple of shops they saw earlier for some of the supplies.

Rigby asked about their parents and other people back home, but Francis assured him that time was different here, so when they were allowed to go back home, they would scarcely notice they even left at all.

Rigby listened to this intently and nodded his head, acknowledging what he heard.

Rigby looked at a table on the piece of instructional paper.

Since he was a starter, he had to get *Math in the Bath* by Brandon Tubb, *Biblical Bible* by Anonymous, and an option from either these four books: *Dragon Slayer* by Miranda Nopew, *Plantology for Starters* by Jorgé Rodriguez, *Spiritual Guidance* by Wriye Tere, or *Making Things that Change the World* by Carey Penter. "Let's hit the bookstore! Wherever that is!" he said.

Francis smirked. He pointed to a tan stucco building across the street from HEB. "It's right here," he joked.

Bolded letters of iron that were stained black said, "Sign of the Time Bookstore." It didn't quite have a solid roof, as did the other buildings in the shopping area. Rather, it had wooden beams that crisscrossed each other topped with bunches of hay. It was fairly big. Considering having hay for a roof, Rigby thought the store owners must need to hire a person just to clean the floor from all the hay that falls.

"All right," Rigby sighed. "Let's go." They walked toward the bookstore.

3

Bad Stuff at the Bank

Only after getting to the door, Francis stopped, realizing the needed some Hadash Edenite currency.

"We don't have any money." Francis said.

Rigby got used to this place quite easily, because he liked adventure. Francis seemed to take a little longer, because he always had a slight stutter in his speech. But for the most part, he seemed all right.

"Right. Where do we get the money? A bank?"

Francis nodded. "I have a little m—money in a local bank, but not enough for the both of us."

Rigby considered this for a moment. "Why don't we swing by the local B of A or something like that?"

Francis frowned. I doubt the—"

But Rigby already started walking toward a building.

The building looked like a commercial structure, except windows made most of the exterior and reflected their surroundings.

Rigby stopped and opened a door at Bank of Christ.

The walls were white and the cubicles lined the left and right walls. The tiles were a dirty white, and a green plant sat by the dark, wooden front desk.

He walked up to the receptionist and asked, "Hey, do you guys have a school fund for starters? Francis here said they do. We're one of the seven kids or whatever."

Francis groaned. Rigby was almost acting like the person in charge.

The lady in the front seemed a little taken back. "You're two of the seven?"

Rigby nodded. But the lady didn't move.

Awkward silence hung in the air.

"Please." Francis added quietly. The lady consented. "Follow me."

They followed her through a series of twists and turns until they finally stopped at a trapdoor at the bottom of the floor.

"Down here," the lady said. She opened the trapdoor and motioned them to go down.

There was a ladder, thankfully. They went down, Rigby in the lead. Once they got down, the stench of sewer drainage filled their nose.

"Holy cow! It reeks!" Rigby said. Francis felt the same, but didn't complain.

Seven pouches filled with money stood hanging on hooks.

"Go ahead and grab a pouch each. Then, you can come up," the lady said.

Rigby and Francis each grabbed a pouch. But as soon as the leather pouch was off a hook, the ground rumbled.

"Goodbye!" the lady said cackling, and she slammed the trapdoor shut, leaving nothing to see but darkness.

"WHAT DO WE DO!?" screamed Francis out of shock. Rigby felt fear for the first time in his life. He was tricked.

The feeling of betrayal was atrocious.

"I—I don't know, Francis!" a crack in the ground split between them. "Grab the money on your side!" Rigby shouted to Francis.

But Francis hesitated and stayed put.

Meanwhile, Rigby made a few daring jumps to get the money for the other seven. He grabbed three others, now holding four. Each pouch weighed a few pounds, so four was heavy when he was trying to run.

"Grab the other two!" cried Rigby, as another crack sliced through the ground, cutting them off, now relying on their only escape spot: the ladder.

"I—I can't!" Francis cried.

Rigby groaned. "Forget it, then. Jump and escape!" Rigby jumped onto the ladder as a crack split the ground with a foot of length in the middle.

He lost one money bag, holding on to the last three of four remaining. Rigby climbed up the ladder, and with all his might, bust the trapdoor open, losing another pouch full of money. He got to the top.

"Francis, NOW!"

Francis ran as fast as he could and jumped onto the ladder as the floor crumbled and fell into the abyss.

"Toss the money!"

Francis did.

Rigby barely caught it because his adrenaline was messing him up.

Francis climbed to the top, his chest heaving in exhaustion. He just made it to the top when the ladder fell.

"Help!" Francis yelled, his hands just hanging on to the top. Rigby set his money bags aside and let his hand out. "Release a hand and grab on!"

Rigby could tell Francis didn't want to. Francis's hand slipped.

"Grab on!" Rigby yelled again.

Francis tried, but he couldn't. He didn't see how long he'd last, either one of them, really.

Rigby reached his hand down as far as he could. *Someone from the bank should be coming,* he thought. Francis grabbed on.

Rigby pulled as hard as he could. His muscles were working overtime now, and he might just fall in with Francis.

But then, he heard running footsteps. Someone pulled Rigby's feet from behind, and he started moving up towards the ground. Francis and he slowly came up. And at last, they were safe up on the ground.

They lay down, catching their breath. Rigby didn't rest for long because he needed to find their rescuer. He looked around and saw many people surrounding them. One person, in a shabby black suit and tie loomed over them. He was tall and lanky and had slightly messy hair.

"H—how did you—" Rigby started.

"Don't worry about that," he said, "just continue what you're doing. I'll inform the Bureau." And he left, his cologne smelling wind giving Rigby's nose a shock.

All the bank workers escorted them out of the bank, and went back to work, glancing at the trapdoor, now with caution tape around it. Rigby put the extra money bags on the floor.

Once they were outside, Rigby tried to shake off the shock. Francis couldn't do it as good. They walked in silence towards the Sign of the Time bookstore. Thankfully, Francis stuffed the paper

Marie gave him, otherwise, it would have gotten lost in the pit.

Rigby took the paper from Francis's pocket, and looked at it.

"Okay," he said shakily, his voice still affected by the incident at the pit, "we need a Biblical Bible, Later Years Edition." They walked a little farther, and entered the bookstore.

4

Dragon Slayer

Rigby's nose immediately smelt new books, and he loved it.

The bookstore was almost exactly like a library. You walk up to the front, go behind the front desk, turn left, and there are all the books you could possibly imagine towards the right. However, this bookstore went by authors only. Normally it would be subject, then author at a regular library. The back was closed off for what looked like new shipments, and the lights were a casual dark yellow that made the wooden shelves look decades old.

Rigby and Francis first started on the left, starting with A. The Biblical Bible was written by Anonymous.

"A. Where is A? Aha!" Francis said. "Biblical Bible, Later Year Edition. Right here, Rigby."

Rigby followed him.

It was a baby blue colored book, about five inches high standing up, similar to the shape of a square. Since it was a Bible that included extra writing technique, the pages were so thin! Rigby looked to the back of the book, and found that this

Bible was two thousand pages long! He was sure it weighed at least twenty pounds, easy.

From the look on Francis's face, he had the same problem. It was too heavy to carry for long, considering they had to buy at least three more books.

When it felt like they couldn't carry it any longer, a chubby man with spiky black hair appeared on a ladder. It moved on wheels connected to a shelf.

"Need some help?" he asked.

Francis and Rigby nodded urgently. "Martha! I need a cart ASAP!" the man yelled. Soon enough, a chubby woman ran over with a small cart.

"Here you are. Drop the books in, Dears!"

They did so.

"Holy Moley!" cried Francis. "I only held this thing for two minutes and I thought I was going to drop it on my toes!"

The lady smiled. "Are both of you the first seven?"

"Yeah."

"I heard what happened at the bank. Are you okay? The city Bureaucracy released a paper a few minutes ago."

They both nodded, though Francis looked skeptical.

"We'll give you a discount on your books because so much of the donations for the seven were lost. We'll give the other seven a discount as well," the man said.

How does the currency work?" asked Francis.

"Seven bronze Noahans equal one silver Starlum. Starli for plural. And four Starli equal one Edenite."

"Okay, thanks, uh, Ms."

The lady looked shocked and looked at the man. "Did you not introduce yourself, Bert?"

He put his hands up and said, "Hey, Martha! I had to help them immediately."

Martha didn't seem pleased and gave a grunt. "Well, I am Martha Owens. And this here is my husband, Bertie Owens."

They each stuck out their hands to shake, which the boys shook.

"I'm Francis," said Francis.

"And I'm Rigby. Rigby Cross."

"I hope you have a good time shopping!" said Mrs. Owens.

"If you need any help, just ask us. We own this store." Said Mr. Owens.

"Thank you," said Francis. And the boys went off for the next book on the list. Going down to the right more, they looked for Tubb, Brandon.

"They seemed nice," Francis stated.

Rigby snorted. "Yeah, those kinds of people who are super nice usually betray the good guys in the horror movies I've watched."

Francis sighed. "I don't know if I should believe you."

"Don't," Rigby said, "well, not all the time. I learned quite a bit from the Warner Brothers.

Those guys who I just talked about, who lie sometimes, are usually the ones who are the best and save people's lives."

"Do you really base your life on these stupid Hollywood pictures!" Francis asked.

Rigby stopped walking and frowned. "You don't?"

Francis left it at that and found the next book. "The book is called *Math in the Bath 2*." Said Rigby. "Did he seriously invent this book while washing in the bath?"

Francis smirked. "I don't even want to know."

It was a green book, not as thick as the Biblical Bible, thankfully. Francis looked at the price. "Two Starli. Hope we're getting a good deal here. I don't know how to convert this to dollars."

Rigby sighed. "Doesn't matter. Mr. Owens said we'd get a discount."

They grabbed two books.

The next book could be whatever they wanted out of a set of books shown. There was a series called *Dragon Slayer* by Miranda Nopew, which was learning how to ward off evil spirits and, obviously, slay dragons. With Rigby's luck, that part would probably be at the end of the last book, or even in the last book of the series.

Another book was called *Plantology*, which Francis snatched up right away without looking at the price. There was a book for starters, learners, apprentices, and graduals. Rigby and Francis were starters, ages eleven through twelve. The boys were both twelve, so Rigby figured they wouldn't have much time to finish their first term.

Spiritual Guidance was written by Wriye Tere and was another option. It was orange with a dove on the front cover.

Rigby looked at the back cover and read it. Basically, it was what you learned from *Dragon Slayer* except this was much lamer. It was somewhat decent, though. It included all the prayers you could imagine, a mass guide, how to use the Holy Spirit, and tips on becoming involved in Holy Orders.

Holy Orders was a sacrament you received if you wanted to become a priest, nun, bishop, archbishop, et cetera, and the priests and higher up in the hierarchy could perform Mass and bless the Holy Eucharist.

The last compulsory option was *Making Things That Change the World* by Carey Penter. This book was about making super cool weapons, tools, and other things. There was even a whole chapter about St. Joseph, the patron saint of workers, in there too.

After all that thinking, Rigby decided to go with *Dragon Slayer*. He could tell it was a popular one, because all the grade levels in this series were on low supply.

Rigby looked at the alternate book options.

Francis didn't want any. He said he'd rather save the money for the other five students enrolling in Hadash Eden Basafel.

Rigby didn't really care though, to be honest. All the optional books were sports, either underwater or on the ground. At first glance, Rigby thought the underwater sport was kind of lame, and the one on the ground which was called Discordance was much more thrilling. But when he read more on Aquatic, he knew this was the kind of sport the world needed.

In Aquatic, you race in an underwater jet-ski thing, called a subracer. The newest model goes a maximum speed of 20mph! You go through obstacle courses throughout the water against two other players, hoping to be the first at the finish.

He grabbed that book and placed it in the cart, though it was expensive. It was 5 starli. Once Rigby and Francis met up again, they headed for the front desk to pay for everything.

"Thanks, boys! Ooh! Plantology, I heard that was a tricky subject." Said Mr. Owens. "No worries, though! When I was in HEB, only the smart kids ever got somewhere with that book!"

He commented on just about every book they bought, hearing a quick ten second story about his years in HEB. "Oho! Dragon Slayer! Back in my day, we had the option to read Defeating Demonic Debacles. I see they replaced it. Oh well."

After that, their total was seven Edenites. "Do you want to try a sample of local guacamole?" Mr. Owens asked.

The boys didn't want to, but they accepted it to be nice.

"Sure, I'll have two." Rigby said.
Mr. Owens handed Rigby and Francis a paper sample bowl. Green, chunky substances with chopped tomatoes were in it. A tortilla chip was in their too.

Rigby took a bite, and never tasted anything better.

"Dude," Rigby said, now eating the guacamole plain, "this is amazing!"

Francis tried it. "Wow! Where did this come from?"

Mr. Owens smiled. "It comes from Holy Molly's Guacamole Shop. Best guac in Hadash Eden!"

Francis frowned. "Holy Moley Guacamole?"

Mr. Owens shook his head. "Holy *Molly's* Guacamole."

Francis smiled. "Ah, okay. I see the point."

"This saying is very common in Hadash Eden. Don't be surprised if you hear it multiple times a day by the same person."

They said bye and left for Joe's General Store.

"HOLY MOLLY'S GUACAMOLE!" Mr. Owens said all of a sudden from behind. Rigby looked back, and Mr. Owens winked.

5
McKinzie Hallow

At the general store, Rigby and Francis constantly lost where they were. There were no signs, no aisle numbers, and no employees in sight. Rigby always thought general stores were stores like Home Depot or Lowes, and sold very similar items. This was exactly the place, except they sold way more items, and locating where they were in the store was nearly impossible.

Rigby figured the store was three times the size of a Home Depot, but he didn't know for sure.

"See any uniform that has something to do with HEB?" Francis asked as they tried another aisle.

Seeing nothing, Rigby replied, "No." His eyes were beginning to hurt, because he kept constantly straining his eyes for some sign of uniform. He wasn't even sure they had clothes here.

"Wait!" Rigby said, spotting something. Francis looked excited.

"I think I— Never mind. Just window drapes."

The boys sighed.

Their trip to the Joe's General Store went something like this a few more minutes, until Francis bumped into somebody.

"Whoops, sorry." Francis mumbled under his breath, without looking up from the paper Marie had given them.

Rigby was behind him, quickly swerving to avoid her bumping into him. He smiled apologetically.

But the girl didn't need to ram into him. She stopped abruptly and said, "Holy Molly's Guacamole! That was rude! I've never seen a man treat a lady with this much disrespect in my whole life!" She looked at Francis, who seemed to have fallen asleep standing up while looking at the paper he was clutching.

She grunted and looked at Rigby. She stared at him for a while, as if she were a scientist examining a specimen to experiment on.

"I'm McKinzie Hallow. Are you with him?" she said swiftly.

"Uh, yeah. Why do you Hadash Edenites say 'Holy Molly?'"

Her face couldn't have displayed more rage than Rigby thought a person could manage.

"It's supposed to be a joke," she muttered.

Francis started moving around looking for items behind McKinzie.

"And do you believe, your ignorant friend here can treat women like that!?" She moved her head like crazy, counting off things on her fingers telling Rigby why he should give a lady more respect.

Rigby faced a hard decision. So, he went with his gut.

"The thing is, my friend here's not a man." She blinked.

This was the kind of game Rigby hated playing: Being a smart Alec.

Three seconds went by in silence. Then another few more seconds. She obviously didn't prepare for that retort.

Francis snuck behind her and took something out of her hand, unnoticed.

"He's a twelve-year-old brainiac adolescent who I dare you to challenge in double Jeopardy!" Rigby threatened. She fumed now.

But she didn't continue. She turned around and whacked her brown hair at Rigby in the face, poking both of his eyes, and turned and left.

"Francis," Rigby said, after his eyes were healing, "next time, be a little more cautious at this place. Especially around girls that call themselves women. We didn't mean any harm. Just be careful."

Francis nodded. "I got something from her though."

"A lesson?" asked Rigby. "Because—"

"No, an object."

"Isn't that stealing?"

Francis shrugged. "Yeah, probably.

Rigby asked for the object. It was a gold coin with a snake coiled around the tree. It was an Edenite. "You stole *money* from her!?" Rigby asked astonished.

"Oh! Uh, I guess. I had a weird feeling when I held the coin, but forgot it when she left."

Rigby frowned. "Of course, you did! You're like a what, twelve-year-old adolescent male!? Of course you lost it when she left!"

But Rigby could tell it was a different feeling than being around a girl. "Maybe it's enchanted," said Francis.

Rigby highly doubted this circumstance, but he listened since Hadash Eden was slightly off from Earth.

"Isn't the Catholic Church totally against enchantments? How can Hadash Eden have magic things?"

Francis shrugged. "Maybe if we asked it to do something, maybe a small favor, it would help us. We need uniforms anyways."

Rigby thought about that. "Don't know nothin' 'till you try. That's for everything."

"Okay, coin. Help us find HEB uniforms." It didn't work. "All right. Find what we desire most at this moment." It still didn't budge.

"You need to say it in Hebrew," said a voice out of nowhere. Francis and Rigby whirled around. They saw a boy about their age come up to them with a sword in his hand.

"RUN!!!" cried Francis. He dove into a kitty litter box right next to a sign that said it was on sale for 10% off. Rigby ran behind a wheel barrow.

The kid frowned. He had dirty blonde hair, wore jeans, and a black t-shirt. His sword was made of rubies and silver. "Oh," he said, like he forgot something. He touched a button at the bottom of his sword, which shrank into a pencil. He stuffed the pencil into his pocket.

"That better?" he asked. Rigby felt safer and came up. Francis came after.

"Do you have an Iserd?" he asked.

"What's an Iserd?" responded Rigby.

"You're part of the seven?"

Rigby was tired of being called "The Seven." "Yeah."

The boy in the black shirt nodded. "An Iserd is a rare object that can guide you to what you need, as long as you say the words in Hebrew. Normally one word is best, but you can't always do that."

37

Rigby saw Francis look more excited. They would find their uniforms before tomorrow!

"Thanks!" said Francis.

"No problem!" the boy responded. "I'm Frank Mason. I'll be a learner this year. If you need any help—well, use your Iserd!"

They said goodbye and started looking for their uniforms in the right direction this time.

Francis pulled out his phone from his pocket and looked up "Find Hadash Eden School Uniforms" in Hebrew. Then he said, "*Leenso Hadash Eden Basafel Medeen*," to the coin. At least that's how it sounded.

Immediately, the coin tugged his arm.

"Ho!" Francis cried as the coin pulled him forward. They had to run to stay in line with the Iserd.

They turned quickly, left and right, and at last arrived in the uniform section.

"Whoa." They said in unison. A whole row consisted of different kinds of uniforms. The male uniforms consisted of navy-blue pants, shiny black dress shoes, and a dark green baggy collared shirt. The shirt had a light blue diamond-arrow symbol inscribed with HEB. And the socks were dark grey. They had a sweater and coat the same color design as the shirt. The boys bought a pair each of one of everything, because they didn't know the weather patterns in Hadash Eden.

Just out of interest, they looked at the girls' uniform. There were dark green or navy-blue skirts just above the knees. The tops were blue with the same HEB symbol on the front. So many different kinds of shoes, socks, and hair supplies were available, eventually they got bored of looking.

Seeing there was nothing else to buy, the boys paid for their items and left to look for a place to stay the night.

6
School of New Eden

It turned out that Rigby and Francis didn't need to find a place to sleep for the night at all; the school opened at midnight. So very happily, they stayed up late and got everything ready for HEB.

Dressed in their new blue and green uniforms, they headed for the school stairs. Older students were allowed to go in, but the new seven were supposed to wait.

Rigby asked the school manager, who happened to be Marie, where all the money and books went. She said she'd already taken care of it, and that it would appear when they learned how to summon it. Rigby hoped he wouldn't be behind on learning how to summon his books, because he was sure to fail without them.

The new seven were supposed to make a grand entering into the Entrance Room where they could also eat once school started.

At last, a few minutes before midnight, all students were inside except for the seven.

"Alright, Seven! Strait line before we enter the Entrance Room!" said a gravelly voice.

A stout man with a peppery beard appeared before them. "We need you to be on your best behavior when entering. Miss Hallow! Shut your mouth! We don't need to know the latest gossip on Justin Bieber!" Two girls around her giggled as McKinzie turned red.

All the boys lined up behind the girls in a single file. One boy who had bright blonde hair looked at his feet nervously. Rigby had a feeling he would get along with Francis well.

"Here, uh, dude," Rigby said, "do you like plantology?" The boy tilted his head a little and nodded. "This guy Francis here seems to like it too. He wants to know a lot about, uh, plants. Come in front of me." He looked surprised, but he went in front of Rigby.

The stout man with a peppery beard told them to be clean and on their best behavior, and other stuff like that.

Minutes later, the doors opened and the starters walked into the cheering crowd in between two long, stone, rectangular tables.

Rigby couldn't believe it. The room was humongous. In the front, a stone slab with five different colored bowls on top of a small stone pillar. On the left, there was a large cafeteria, and on the right was a skinnier stone table where the teachers ate and sat.

The large, plump man signaled them to sit at the middle-right table.

Once the cheering died down, another man who was middle aged stood up and cleared his throat. His black hair covered his forehead, and he had black facial whiskers.

"Thank you everyone for the applause and gratitude for the starters. My name is Mr. Highten, HEB's superintendent and principal. Before we go to bed tonight, I must tell you a few reminders. You are not allowed to visit the rest of Hadash Eden unless supervised by a teacher. However, your teachers may escort you to the motel when it is time.

"Nine o'clock is bedtime. Any person out of bed or the motel will receive twice the homework assigned by your teachers for a month. Good luck with that.

"And for something more fun, we may begin the effort to Opt the new starters. When your name is called, come up to the front steps. There will be five bowls in front of you. Each one represents a certain Opt. Sagacious the intelligent, Valiant the brave, Diffident the reserved, Munificent the selfless, and Vigorous the mighty, are the opts. Once you are in the circle, images will flash in your mind. You might see a cute baby turtle, or a unicorn goring you with its horn! Complete what needs to be done. There will be images that can help you pick the bowl. Then, pick the bowl! You will receive letters delivered that reveal your opt in about a week or so."

Rigby frowned. He had no idea what opt meant, so he decided to consult Francis next to him. "Francis, what does 'opt' mean?"

But Francis didn't hear Rigby; he was too busy talking about what they might learn about in plantology with his new friend, Matthew. Matthew was the boy with very blonde hair.

So very unwillingly, Rigby had to figure it out the hard way.

"Claudia Jubilee!" said Mr. Highten. A happy eleven-year-old girl with frizzy black hair walked up to the front of the Entrance Room. She climbed the stairs and stood in the circle of five bowls. Immediately, she tensed. A couple starters gasped, but the rest of the school just sighed.

She kept saying random words like "No" and "I told you, I can't do it! I can prove it! Help!" Some of the words were so unnerving, some learner had to hold some scared starters down.

At last, she stopped and picked the bowl in the middle, which seemed like she was doing so in a trance. Yellow flames shot upward and died at the roof from the bowl.

A teacher named Ms. Abble had to escort her back to the table. Another girl went up and did similar things, with escorting. McKinzie Hallow, the girl who was extremely biased to manly manners, was up next. Rigby couldn't wait to see her shout and scream and do whatever the other girls did. Rigby wanted revenge. He hoped stealing her Iserd wasn't bad karma though.

But instead, she didn't scream or shout. She actually did the opposite. She looked confident and wasn't afraid to back down. She even did a cartwheel-kick thing, which should've knocked a couple stone bowls off their stands, but apparently, they were permanently stuck.

Red flames shot upward from the bowl.

She stopped abruptly and didn't need help going back, though it seemed like she needed it. Her face turned a slight shade of green, but most people just shrugged it off.

Francis and Matthew looked nervous when they went up to the circle, but they might have enjoyed it. "Ha! I told you transcription is when DNA turns into RNA!" and stuff like that. Those two were the last to Opt other than Rigby.

"Rigby Cross!" Mr. Highten called.

Rigby stood up and walked slowly to the front in the circle of stone bowls.

This time, unlike all the others, gas erupted from the bowls. First, orange, then pale green and black. They went back and forth, changing colors and took forms as horses riding around the whole room.

I don't think this is supposed to happen, Rigby thought, scared. Mr. Highten stood up and shouted at Rigby, telling him to get down from the stairs. But he couldn't hear him.

Fire circled around him, letting obnoxious scents of death and decay in his nose. The gases were too much, and he collapsed into an illusion.

He was riding a large black mare on an open plane. The grass swayed gently in the breeze as the sun set in the distance. It was a peaceful sight. Rigby had never been to the country, but this was exactly how he imagined it would be. He had no idea how to ride a horse, but suddenly he knew.

Up ahead, he saw a big red barn. He had a feeling that this barn was his home, so he decided to bring the horse into a trot. Rigby didn't know if he was sharing a mind with the horse, but if so, he didn't mind.

Once in the barn, he put the horse into her stall, but she wouldn't listen.

45

She reared and bucked and whinnied. She was so strong; Rigby lost his grip on her halter and she reared once more. But this time, it turned into a huge, gigantic snake that was coiled in front of Rigby.

"Riiiby Crosss." The snake said. It then transformed into a large red dragon. Scared out of his wits, Rigby ran away from the barn, but the dragon caught up to him. It breathed fire on the grass, setting a wildfire across the plain.

Rigby ran and tried to find something he could fight the dragon with, but he couldn't find anything. "You will be devoured by the Accuser, Valiant!" the dragon said. "We will return!"

The fire now surrounded him in a circle, slowly closing in on him. The dragon towered above him, flying malevolently in the air. Just when Rigby thought he was going to get engulfed by the flames, he saw a large grandfather clock in the distance, coming closer to him. As the clock came closer, the dragon receded. As soon as the fire touched him, he awoke.

He was dripping sweat in the circle of bowls.

This time, there were no fiery horses that smelled like sewer water.

He got up shakily and sat back down on the stone table. Eyes followed him eerily all the way to the table and sat upon him.

Some whispered, "Is that the guy who almost died at the bank?"

"Rigby Cross!" A voice boomed. Mr. Highten stood up and looked at him, which made Rigby stop in his tracks. "In my office. Now."

7
Spiritual Defense

Rigby followed Mr. Highten to his office. He sat down in a chair opposite of his principal.

The room was very bland, but Rigby could tell there was much history inside, concealed. There were bookshelves surrounding the whole room aside from the door. There were occasional trinkets of globes and other antiques like a grandfather clock and teacups. The grandfather clock seemed to radiate a powerful feeling toward Rigby. He would know more later.

Then Mr. Highten spoke. "What did you see?" He demanded.

Rigby shuffled uncomfortably.

"I had a dream. More like a warning illusion." And then Rigby told him what happened.

The only sound Mr. Highten made while Rigby spoke was grunts and gasps. When Rigby finished, there was a few minutes of silent, deep thinking from Mr. Highten. At last, Rigby broke out full of questions.

"Did I do something wrong?"

Mr. Highten gave him a stern look. "Did you try to do something wrong?"

"No." Rigby responded.

"Then did you do something wrong?" Mr. Highten said.

Rigby nodded no, answering his own question.

"If you believe you didn't do something wrong, and deep down inside your soul you truly didn't do anything wrong, then why did you ask me?" Rigby nodded once more, understanding his thinking.

"This illusion you had is a sign coming from God, no doubt. However, normally he gives us clues to the clues for the remedy to prevent catastrophes. Similar things have occurred, I've had a few myself, but this specific one seems a little more calamitous. However, it seems this illusion you had is a very clear warning. A clock that you found in the field, seems to be the only way, or most effective way to prevent a mass attack. That mass attack is what the wildfire is, I suppose."

He raised an eyebrow at Rigby. "Are you with me?"

Rigby nodded sleepily.

He had no idea what the heck he was talking about. It was past midnight, after all, and Rigby always had a short attention span. Also, he wasn't a mastermind on interpreting dreams or illusions or whatever. Nor did he believe that it was an art that

49

should be practiced, most likely because of his bad experience with interpreting them.

One night, Rigby dreamed of a dog barking happily with delight and him playing fetch with it. According to his dream guide, that meant he would receive social recognition. A week or two later, a friend's dog died. The outcome was completely irrelevant to the prediction. In another instance, Rigby dreamt of an empty keg bottle in front of him. That supposedly meant that he would have prosperity. He had no idea where that came from, though his dad and him went past a rowdy bar one Saturday night to get to a bowling alley. The next day, he received an F on alcoholic fermentation in science. As you can see, Rigby didn't care a thing about interpreting dreams. He believed it was just memories that you had the past week coming up again.

"As for the fiery horses and stench," Mr. Highten continued, "that could mean death and plague. I learned that in Revelation."

Rigby nodded.

"This talk never happened. Do you understand?"

"Yes."

"I need you to write your dreams down a piece of paper every time you have them. Is that clear?"

"Yes."

"Goodnight."

Rigby walked out of the room, and followed the plump man to the motel for sleep.

The next day, Rigby and Francis walked into the school after getting ready for the day.

A poster in the Entrance Room was hung by the teachers' table. It stated:

Starters' List for the Week
1.Math in the Entrance Room 9:00
2.Bible studies in Entrance Room 10:00
3.Lunch break 11:30
4.Spiritual Defense/Plantology/Craftsmanship
12:30
5.Aquatic Options 2:00
Notes: Summoning powers must be completed today.

It was eight 'o'clock, so Rigby and Francis had an hour before their first class. Rigby figured math and Bible studies were boring, but everything after that looked fun. He took Spiritual Defense instead of plantology or craftsmanship, because he liked weapons. He didn't know what options for Aquatic there was, but he figured he should at least show up.

Breakfast went by fast, aside from avoiding McKinzie's glances at him, looking for the Iserd.

When she didn't look, both Francis and him shuddered.

At math class, they didn't do much math. They had to practice summoning their books. Rigby got the hang of it after his one hundred and fifty-sixth try. That was an amazing amount, compared to Claudia Jubilee. She incorrectly summoned her book, only retrieving the front cover.

In Bible studies, most of the class summoned their books correctly. Well, the right pages at least.

Francis asked where the books were before they summoned them, and Mr. Gravelbard, the plump man with the peppery beard, said it was stored in an intermediate realm between Heaven and Earth. That was an astounding answer to most students.

They learned about the creation, and how it tied in with evolution. Interestingly, Mr. Gravelbard made Rigby and the class to decide for themselves whether evolution or creation or both combined was true, instead of just telling them what it is.

At lunch, Rigby met up with Francis who brought Matthew along. Rigby was getting jealous of Matthew, stealing his friend Francis, but Rigby had been equally wrong, trying to take popularity from him.

Rigby was starting to realize how dumb he was for wanting popularity.

Before twelve-thirty, Rigby set off for Spiritual Defense. He took a left turn in the Entrance Room up the stairs. He walked a few more paces, until he came across a shiny brown door. A sign on the door wrote Spiritual Defense. Rigby walked in.

The front of the classroom had a chalkboard with complex drawings, and the middle of the classroom had long, marble desks for about five people a table. There were four of these. In the back, swords, shields, prayer cards, and even a scarecrow with a pumpkin head lay on a mini table.

This time, he was with some older students too.

"Sit down," came a gravelly voice. Rigby silently groaned.

It was Mr. Gravelbard. His voice was really annoying, and it was hard to concentrate when Mr. Gravelbard talked. Not only was it hard to concentrate, but he made everyone jot notes down very quickly, which always made Rigby's hand hurt.

Once in Bible studies, Mr. Gravelbard said, "Parts of creation are actually evolution." But Rigby couldn't quite understand him that well while writing his notes, so it came out like "Farts of vacation are actually the solution." Rigby didn't realize he wrote it in his Bible until after Francis's snot flew onto his book from laughing.

"Hello, Rigby. Take a seat." Rigby went to the very front table so that if Mr. Gravelbard wrote notes, Rigby could always read it if he was behind.

Other students piled in soon enough, and their lesson begun. Rigby didn't realize Frank Mason was sitting next to him until he nodded his head. *What's up?* he seemed to say. Rigby mimicked it.

Frank pointed to a boy near him. "That's Thomas," he said. "He's very quiet, but he's very smart."

Thomas was a goofy kid with brown, messy hair and brown eyes. He was somewhat skinny, and had freckles around his nose

"Hello students," Mr. Gravelbard began. "Welcome to this year's first Spiritual Defense lesson. Mondays and Wednesdays will be textbook days—"

"—Uhhhhhh," everyone sighed.

"I hate the textbook. I want to actually do something," Frank whispered.

Rigby was excited. At St. Anne's, all he did was textbook work.

"As I was saying," Mr. Gravelbard continued, with reproving looks at his students, "Those are the textbook days. Tuesday and Thursday will be hands on. Starters and learners will be working on killing

Serplandi this week. The learners will be attempting to kill especially feisty ones—"

"Ooh!" came voices nearby Frank. He was smiling.

"Apprentices, you will leave for Outyard next week, so you'll just be learning how to kill dragons in the textbook this year. And last but not least, graduals will be learning the big thing but practicing on mini versions: Killing dragons."

Cheers erupted from all around.

Under the noise, Rigby asked Frank, "What's the Outyard?"

Frank sighed. "Nobody really knows for sure. It's basically the land beyond the known boundaries of Hadash Eden. It's a place full of big surprises, but not all of them are wanted. We lost an apprentice last year on that field trip to a rogue spirit ranting and raving about clocks."

There it was again. The clock. It always seemed to come up. Rigby needed more information. He decided not to press Frank though. He didn't want him to be suspicious.

Frank shivered, but sat taller. "On the bright side, if you save someone from a demon or something like that, you can get serious accomplishments on your resume. It will help you get a good Spiritual-Defense-like job."

"All right, graduals and apprentices, I need you to grab R2D2s and go outside." A handful of students got up and grabbed some weapons from the back table and went outside with booming voices.

"Is Mr. Gravelbard talking about R2D2 from Star Wars?" Rigby asked Frank.

Frank sighed. "Dang, kid. I forgot how *new* some starters could be. R2D2 stands for Range 2 and Danger 2. It basically means a spear that is the Danger 2 model, and size two. The lower the number, the longer the spear. Another famous weapon was the Range 7 Danger 4. Most powerful spear of its day."

Mr. Gravelbard turned his back to the remaining students and said, "Open to page four in *Dragon Slayer*. Frank, read the heading, 'Serplandi Weaknesses.'"

It appeared Mr. Gravelbard liked Frank a lot, because he read half of a whole chapter which was about five pages long.

Frank hadn't said a word for the rest of class because his mouth was as dry as the desert.

In that day's lesson, Rigby learned Serplandi were tiny snakes that lived in the plain burrows and were very common in Hadash Eden. Their bight is lethal, but you have to hurt them really bad before they think about attacking you. They live on Earth, but most people overlook them as worms because they don't have HEB knowledge.

"For the next part in our lesson, we will be learning Latin," Mr. Gravelbard said.

Rigby raised his hand. "Why do we need to learn Latin?"

Mr. Gravelbard smirked. "Are you a Catholic?"

"Yeah," Rigby responded. "Does Latin help with Spiritual Defense then?"

Mr. Gravelbard nodded. "It is very important actually. You can command your weapon to do certain things."

Frank smiled and nodded his head like this was the best thing in the world.

Mr. Gravelbard went to the back of the room and grabbed a sword and book for each student, which was about ten or so each.

Rigby grasped the hilt and set it down in front of him. They were deadly looking.

"The first step of commanding your weapon, in this case, a sword, is obviously learning Latin.

"To begin, you start with its name. Then, give it a command. If you need to give it an adverb, which you should only do rarely, do it lastly. Imagine your weapon is a machine. You can't work it too hard and not expect it to work, break, or blow up on you."

Rigby raised his eyebrows. "Blow up, Mr. Gravelbard?" Rigby asked nervously. Mr. Gravelbard nodded gravely.

"Anyways, unless a sword was given a specific name while being forged by craftsmen—"

"Or craftswomen," a female voice said.

"Yes, okay. If so, you will just call your sword the word sword, spear, spear, et cetera, et cetera."

"What are some of the commands?" Thomas asked.

"Some are 'aim,' 'slice,' 'puncture,' and even 'return.' The adverbs are 'mistakenly,' 'slowly,' 'swiftly,' 'stealthily,' and there's others just to name a few.

This was a lot of information for Rigby. But it was still fun to learn.

Then Mr. Gravelbard said, "Watch me as an example." He stepped back and aimed his hand for Frank Mason's sword. "Gladius, cito redi." he said. Immediately, the sword flew toward him and into his fingers.

"Whoa," voices said.

"Read this section in *Dragon Slayer* for homework." Mr. Gravelbard said. "Class is dismissed."

After Spiritual Defense, Rigby remembered that Aquatic Options started at two 'o'clock. Rigby raced to the pool, well, *lake*. That's how big it was. There were many students older than Rigby was. Most were comprised of learners and graduals, because the apprentices were always on field trips and starters were only allowed to practice with the team. Francis came, but only to watch.

"Welcome, everyone!" the Aquatic instructor said. He had a muscular frame and blonde hair. "Hello, Coach Sirump!" the students said.

"Let me explain the basics of Aquatic for everyone. First of all, I need you all to finish the first chapter in *Aquatic for Newbs* if you haven't. It's pretty basic, just going over the history and rules of the game. Anyways, practice is twice a week, Monday and Wednesday at two. Starters, HEB has a rule that you can't play any sports until next year, but if you can be really, really good, then I can always persuade Mr. Highten so you can play for HEB!

"All right!" he said. "Let's put our Aquatic suits on, so we can talk and breathe underwater. Just the basics."

A short girl with dark hair and purple highlights next to Rigby smirked. "I've been practicing Aquatic for years. I bet I can beat just about everyone here. What do you think?" she asked Rigby, with a slight bit of dare in her voice.

"Uh, I don't know how good you are, but it sounds like your good." Normally at St. Anne's, he would unleash a load of nasty retorts in a fury to people like that. But here, he knew to never underestimate somebody. Who knew, maybe she had an invisible sword and knew a lot of Latin. Rigby didn't want to be a victim of sword that understood Latin.

"Hmph," she said. "I know I'm right. I'm Sassina Cawter. Most people call me Sass. What's yours?"

"I go by Rigby," he said.

"What's your real name?" she asked with a slight annoyance.

"Rig," he said, trying to impress his name.

Sass raised her eyebrow, possibly unconvinced. "Whatever, Rig," she said.

Everyone put their scuba diving-like suits on. Frank Mason had to help Rigby put his on.

"Coach Sirump used to play for the eels," Frank said. "If you don't know what that is, it's a professional aquatic team. He won two championships in his twenties, and one in his thirties. He retired at age forty, but still wanted to do more aquatic. Now, he teaches."

"Wow, dang," Rigby said.

"I know, right? His fans called him Three-sixty, for his awesome spinners. Those are spins in a obstacle."

"Does that mean we're gonna be good?" Rigby asked.

Frank laughed. "If you put in the work, yeah."

They dove into the water. At the bottom, the students saw a few underwater jet skis.

"These are called subracers." Said Coach Sirump. "We have the newest model, called the Morrose TQ."

A lot of underwater gasps sounded from the older students. "It has speeds up to twenty miles per hour, and has a built-in waterproof screen for you trackcode." More gasps occurred.

"A trackcode allows the subracer to recognize the track you're on, giving you a navigation and helpful tips through the obstacles. The Morrose TQ has a colorful digital screen, while the Lightspeeds and Swifthastes have a black numbered screen.

"There are three obstacles that you must pass, following the dotted line on your screen. Don't try short cuts either, because Greggory Unfort was sent to the hospital a year ago, and still hasn't improved." Rigby could tell a lot of excitement plummeted. Greggory Unfort must've been a former player that was well known.

The Coach just talked about a few more things, answering quick questions from the starters, and clarifying a few rules. After that, it was 3:30, and the class ended.

The starters didn't have much homework, aside from summoning, answering a few questions on creation versus evolution, and for Rigby, reading the first chapter on Aquatic for Newbs.

Francis and Matthew finished before dinner, and Rigby still had to do reading at the motel. Rigby decided to abandon reading to go look for information about the small grandfather clock.

So, at night, he sneaked into the library to find out more about the clock.

He passed the Boys' rooms in HEB, and entered the library. Ms. Emaciat was the librarian and custodian of the school, and unfortunately, it was rumored that she could spot anyone lurking in the shadows. She was skinny and bony, and looked like she had only one meal a day.

Thankfully, there were no lights on in the library other than Ms. Emaciat's reading light, and Rigby's clothes were dark enough to possibly pass undetected through the darkness.

He slipped passed rows of books and paused every time Ms. Emaciat turned the page. When he looked for the section on clocks, he had no luck.

There were grandfather clocks in some of the readings, but they were just old antiques in the nineteenth century.

After an hour in the library, he went back to the motel and read.

I'll have to ask Francis about the clock, thought Rigby.

He loved the thrill of being away from his parents. Not that he was doing anything wrong, it was just fun.

Sometimes, he would get homesick, but aside from that, he was totally fine. Francis, on the other hand, seemed a little homesick.

Rigby loved this school. He couldn't wait for more.

8

Opt Results

A week later, the Opting results came in at breakfast time. It was delivered by Mr. Heighten's white dove, envelope by envelope. When Rigby was in his office, he never saw a cage at all, so this dove must be new.

"I hope I get Sagacious," said Francis, while munching on a piece of bacon.

"Mmm?" Rigby said through a mouthful of waffles, "'Ut 'efen duf 'at 'ean?"
Francis raised an eyebrow. "You don't know the Opting Theory?"

Rigby gulped some water down. "I don't know any theory. Except ones I forgot."

Francis sighed. "When you went up to the circle of bowls and collapsed and whatever, that was Opting. You were just different from everyone else. You get placed in a certain group, depending upon how you think and act. Sagacious are known, smart and wise. Valiants are brave and foolish, Diffident, humble and quiet, while Vigorous are strong and Munificent are selfless and abnegate to self wants. I don't know, but we might get extra classes about our Opt. They teach you how to think or act better, because they somewhat know how your mind works."

Rigby nodded, taking in only half of what he said. "I hope I get whatever I need to get," said Rigby.

Francis laughed. "Don't worry, Mr. Highten seems to know what he's doing."

Speaking of Mr. Highten, Rigby forgot about writing his dreams down. Of course, nobody could remember all of their dreams a week or more in a row, but Rigby did have one that he only remembered parts from it. It obviously wasn't that important, considering he forgot most of it.

At last, the dove came and gently dropped the envelope by Francis. Matthew came up, and took a seat next to him. Francis rubbed the dove affectionately, and the dove flew off. He opened the envelope, and it said:

Dear Francis Dren,

Thank you for cooperating and participating in Opting. After your test, you have tested positive for Sagacious. The Sagacious are wise, intelligent, and learnt. As one of them, you will be inclined to know much more than most people you come across. This is an obvious trait, either you have recognized it by now, or you haven't. Furthermore, congratulations.

Sagacious training will be on Monday at 3:00 pm on the discordance field.

Thank you so
much,
Mr. Highten

Francis skimmed his eyes over it a few more times. "Sheesh." Rigby said. "It sounds like one of those health videos in fifth and sixth grade."

"Yeah," Francis continued, ignoring him. "I get that vibe too. Whatever, the point is across."

Matthew and Rigby nodded.

"What did you Opt?" Francis asked Matthew.

"What? Oh! Me! I got Diffident. Their reserved and keep to their own things rather than others."

That is Matthew to the T, Rigby thought.

Suddenly, a shriek erupted from across their table. Heads looked in that direction. Claudia Jubilee was in the middle of it reading an envelope. "I got Munificent!" she shrieked happily. Everyone scowled and went back to their seats.

McKinzie Hallow gave another look at them and passed them, most likely looking for her missing Iserd. Rigby and Francis started to quickly have a peculiar liking for their breakfast foods.

"This bacon is splendid," Francis said.

Rigby nodded and responded, "It's so good, I want to eat more. I hope I don't get cardiac arrest.

"You mean cardiopulmonary arrest," Francis said.

"Sure."

Once she passed, Rigby asked, "Do you still have the Iserd?"

Francis gulped. "Yeah. Do you think I should return it?"

Rigby nodded. "Don't deliberately give it back to her though. Put it in her food next time or something."

Then, another boy who was also a starter came up to sit with them, this time next to Rigby. Rigby had never seen this kid before, but Francis and Matthew seemed to know about him. He had jet black hair, combed, and wore a mischievous smile across his face.

"Hey guys," he said casually. "Hi, Barb." Said Francis and Matthew.

A few girls came out from somewhere and came up to Barb. "Would you like to sit next to me in Math?" one of them said.

Barb grinned. "Sure thing!" They giggled and left.

Embarrassed for not knowing him, Rigby stuck out his hand for him to shake. "Hi, nice to meet you. Sorry I haven't come across you yet. I'm Rigby."

Barb pondered that for a moment. Rigby wondered if this pause was socially acceptable. Just when Rigby was going to leave, Barb said, "Rigby, you're Rigby Cross? The person who survived the bank incident!?"

Rigby nodded uncomfortably.

Barb nodded admiringly.

The dove came over the table again, this time coming toward Rigby. He was glad, because he felt a little left out, not being Opted at all yet. The dove dropped an envelope with a "HEB" green stamp on the back. Rigby didn't give the dove any thought at all, so noticing this, the dove ruffled its feathers and flew away. He tore open the letter, revealing the inside.

To his utter disappointment, the letter said nothing. There was no address or sign at all of who wrote the letter. Rigby felt anger boiling and he threw the papers on the ground and didn't talk to anyone for the rest of the day. Nor did he see Barb.

He couldn't believe there was nothing written at all.

The next day, Ms. Emaciat didn't clean the crumbled paper. It was in the same exact spot since yesterday. Everywhere else it was clean. He picked up the rest of the paper and shoved it in his pant pockets, to deal with later.

At night after all his Algebra, Genesis, and Spiritual Defense homework were finished, Rigby took out the pieces of paper. He arranged the pieces back in order, not knowing why he was doing so. It took him about thirty minutes when it was fully completed, taped and all.

There has to be some kind of message in here, thought Rigby. *If only I could decode it.*

Then Rigby saw something.

Letters were appearing in ink on the paper! Rigby watched slowly as the message was revealed. It wrote:

Dear Rigby Cross,

Further research has been conducted by me, Mr. Highten, who has uncovered your Opt. The dragon in your dream, I believe, called you Valiant. You and your fellow Valiants are brave, courageous, and sometimes stupid, due to the fact you are willing put yourself at risk. Normally you would be having lessons with a Valiant teacher, but you won't. I will be teaching you after dinner because it appears to me that this school will face catastrophic consequences if we are unprepared for specific practices. Ironically, I happen to be one. Remember to keep your dream record, and if you get caught trying to come to my office, say you are seeking a book for Spiritual Defense. My office is behind the little library in the Boys' Rooms.

With regard,
Mr. Highten

Rigby was excited. He was going to have special lessons from Mr. Highten! But he wondered why the message only showed up when he was alone. Mr. Highten most likely wanted the message to be concealed, considering he was going to give him secret lessons.

The next day, Rigby couldn't stop thinking about the grandfather clock in Mr. Highten's office. He didn't know why, but it really bothered him. Not only was it in his mind, it was in his dreams. He slept through most of Math and Bible Studies, which didn't surprise him, since he was now becoming a 70% student.

After school, he asked everyone he knew about a special grandfather clock. Ms. Abble, who taught math, was the only one who seemed to avoid that question when he asked. But most people stared at Rigby like he was in La-La Land.

At last, before bed, Rigby asked Francis when Matthew was asleep: "Have you seen a strange grandfather clock at all?"

Francis frowned. "No."

"Can you find out anything about a magical-like grandad clock or something? Maybe in the library?"

"Why?"

"I had a bad dream…" and Rigby told Francis about the illusion he told Mr. Highten on his first day in Hadash Eden. He also backed up Francis with possible evidence, because he was one of those people who don't believe anything without some kind of evidence.

"I know it's weird, but I felt a weird desire to use it for something, something big."

Francis nodded, considering that. Rigby sensed that Francis wouldn't want to do it, no matter how easy it'd be, because it could be risky.

To end the conversation, Rigby said, "It's probably okay to look for—thanks! And goodnight!" He turned his head on his pillow and pretended to fall asleep.

"Whaa? Fine. Fine, Rigby. Goodnight," Francis responded.

Rigby secretly smiled.

9
An Aquatic Race

A week later, Rigby had finally finished *Aquatic for Newbs*. It was an easy read, aside from having to memorize the techniques on how to turn your subracer upside-down while gunning the engine at top speed. This was called a spinner. It was necessary to learn because random currents would appear at the Creepy Current obstacle without notice.

After Spiritual Defense, Rigby ran toward the lake. The class ended late because Rigby read very slow after he had to substitute reading for Frank. Frank had lost his voice.

By the time he had arrived at the lake, everyone was already geared up in their black and green neon aquatic suits.

Rigby quickly suited up and hobbled after everyone submerging into the lake.

He quickly noticed Sass, who undoubtedly recognized him. She made a weird expression, which might have been a scowl, but was hard for him to tell when she had her head in an underwater helmet.

"Welcome again, kids, to this practice." Coach Sirump said.

A few figures crossed their arms and a few bubbles came from their helmets.

Coach Sirump must've been really good a recognizing movement because he said, "Oh, suck it up! You graduals are mostly only eighteen!"

The graduals said, "Yeah, eighteen means we're adults." Like it was obvious, Coach Sirump paid no attention to it.

"Since we have finished reading Aquatic for Newbs, we're going to fully work on racing." He said. "This race includes the Rugged Rocks—" mixed groans and cheers came from the group of students.

"—Humongous Whale's Innards—" Everyone groaned.

"—And Creepy Current. Each obstacle will be about ten to fifteen minutes long." He looked around the crowd. "I will pick three people for a practice race."

Gasps and murmurs rippled through the group. "The first person will be Sassina Cawter, who will get to race the Morrose TQ." A few people cheered her on as she swam through the water heading toward the subracer beside the Coach. She winked at Rigby.

Rigby grimaced through his helmet visor; he wanted to race. But he still had a chance.

"The next person will be a learner," the Coach said. Almost everyone sighed. "Frank, your good. You'll ride a Swifthaste 03."

The Swifthaste looked like a jet ski, except it was made of wood, and there was only a wooden stick that could be used to turn. You had to shift a lot of weight on it to turn. A little metal handle was on the side for breaking, though it either worked too well or not enough for the most part. A little tiny, purple propeller stuck out from the back.

A surprised Frank swam up to the Swifthaste. He got on and started the engine.

"Our last person will be riding another Swifthaste 03. Who wants to race?"

A few people jumped up in the water demanding attention, while others pushed everyone else around. It soon became an all-out brawl. Rigby was mostly trying to avoid it, but got pummeled once or twice by a fist.

All of this happened while Coach Sirump just stood there, watching.

Rigby dodged a couple of kicks, and noticed Sass and Frank were already lining up to race while Coach Sirump helped.

If he could sneak through the crazy amount of people fighting, maybe Rigby could get on the subracer before they took off.

Too late, they took off. But he could still catch up.

He swam as fast as his body would've allowed. He was going to make it! His fingers were practically on it!

He jumped on it and flipped the lever to turn the engine on. The engine growled, but unfortunately, caught others' attention. They swam toward him like a bullet.

Rigby quickly turned on the trackcode. Thank You for Riding SWIFTHASTE, it said. Rigby groaned. *This is not going fast enough*, he though urgently.

The students were fifty yards away.

He had no idea why Coach Sirump was allowing this brawl for racing rights continue.

He looked on the screen and read. Input trackcode _ _ _ _ _

Rigby flicked the lever up eight times for H.

The students were forty yards away.

The lever was flicked up five times, and then twice for the next spot. He got three letters out of five. HEB

He needed two more. "Zero, and then one. Yes!"

They were twenty yards away. Accept trackcode? The trackcode said.

"Yes, yes, yes!"

He flicked the lever up once. Calculating…

They were ten yards away.

Proceed? He flicked it up again.

Everyone was less than two yards away.

Advance. Rigby slammed his foot onto the pedal. He zoomed away as fast as it could let him.

He made sure to count to one hundred before he looked back. Fortunately, no sign of anybody was there.

He breathed a sigh of relief for the first time today.

He looked at his trackcode. It showed a digital map of his course to complete, along with the other players. Black dots represented Sass and Frank, though it wouldn't show who was who. A long line showed the recommended path for Rigby to take.

"Old school tech," Rigby muttered, wanting more advice and detail on the trackcode. By old school, he meant five to ten years ago.

A sign flickered past. Rigby couldn't read it, so he hoped he wasn't veering off course. But according to his trackcode, he was fine.

Up ahead, he saw large, massive rocks. There was a chasm that led to a little light, so Rigby went through there, pulling slightly on the brake.

To his dismay, it shuddered to a complete stop. He gunned the engine again, which propelled him forward.

He wove through multiple cracks, crevices, and chasms that made him almost bump his head on a rock.

All of a sudden, a large, rock statue of St. Junipero Sera stood before him. Rigby angled his subracer to a complete stop and pulled on the brake as much as he could.

It almost threw him off, but instead he slammed his head into the wooden stick. A slight crack appeared in it, which wasn't good.

Fighting the urge to puke, Rigby noticed an inscription below the foot of the Saint. It said, "Those who tear down the statues of me, will feel God's wrath and misfortunes of thee."

Rigby turned his subracer left and went top speed away.

Seeing light up ahead, Rigby finally exited the Rugged Rocks.

Farther down, a subracer disappeared into the mouth of a live whale where there was no water.

"No way," Rigby muttered.

His trackcode showed him going through a large rectangle. *The rectangle must be the whale. Coach Sirump wasn't joking about whale innards.* He thought.

At full speed, he entered the whale's mouth and continued down its throat.

It suddenly grew really dark, and Rigby couldn't see. Then, a light appeared on the front part of the stick of the Swifthaste.

"Dude," Rigby said. "Amazing. I wish I could do that on my forehead or something."

The Swifthaste randomly lurched. Rigby looked back and saw the propeller had shifted from horizontal to up. *It can fly.*

The air around him grew thick, and the wall was a light red. *This must be the esophagus.*

Since the esophagus was fairly straight, he pushed his foot down all the way on the pedal for top speed, about fifteen miles per hour.

Five minutes later, he reached a large, round bowl. The propeller stopped, and he fell into a large, disgusting, wet lake.

He plunged into it, making a splash. Using his trackcode as his only sense of direction, he plunged and went through a lot of thick acid and half broken-down food. Rigby could smell the stench through his helmet, which wasn't good.

His subracer then stopped abruptly, sinking into the sewage. "No, no, no, no!" he yelled. His ride can't die! He pressed the pedal down over and over again, until he gave up. There had to be better ways.

Why did it stop? Was it overworked? Did something get caught in the propeller? *Maybe that.*

He got off of his subracer, moving slowly through the stomach acids and food, and looked at the propeller. Little tiny creatures were stuck in it. Rigby pulled them out, finding that they were already gone, and tried the engine again. It worked.

He raced out of there at top speed.
After the stomach, the way started to become twists and turns. This was the entrance to the intestines.

It was easy for the most part, but then the small intestines arrived. There, he saw Frank.

Rigby slowly caught up. "Are you in second!?" Rigby said over the engines.

Frank nodded. "Yeah," he said.

Rigby smiled. "Not anymore!" he shifted his weight forward and slightly sped up in front of Frank.

A turn came up, and Frank stole the inside and took the lead. Rigby gritted his teeth. The next turn, Rigby took the inside turn and propelled himself forward, only for Frank to tie with him again.

Light came up ahead. Rigby had to get there fast, otherwise it would be hard to catch up to Frank in the Creepy Current.

They went faster, and faster, and even more so! Rigby was now starting to worry. Would he get stuck with Frank at the rear end of the whale? They were now twenty yards away. Ten, five… Rigby pushed the subracer forward as fast as he could.

All of a sudden, a low, grumbling noise echoed in the intestines. The boys feared the worst might happen.

Rigby looked behind him, and a green, gaseous cloud was heading straight for him.

"AHHHHH! NOT A FART!" he screamed.

Then, Rigby was blasted far out of the whale a whole mile into the ocean. He didn't see Frank in front of him.

The power was enough to force him to hold his breath.

Once recovered from the shock, Rigby yelled. "WOOHOO! Who lives to survive a tale like this! Wait 'till I tell Francis!"

Then, something tugged him and his subracer, followed by speeding bubbles. It was the first current. Rigby Cross had entered the Creepy Current, the hardest obstacle in Aquatic.

Random lines of bubbles were everywhere. Those were the currents.

All he had to do was avoid getting caught in one, and follow the line on his trackcode. Then he'd win. But unfortunately, the currents tugged you towards them.

Rigby sped around the currents, and spotted Sass. She seemed as if she had no trouble.

After avoiding a few more currents, he caught up to her. She seemed surprised, but quickly masked it with a scowl.

"Let's see if you can stand your ground against me," she said. That was easy to do.

Then she added, "While I push you." That was not easy to do.

She rammed the brand new Morrose TQ right into Rigby's Swifhaste. He just barely dodged a current.

Seeing she missed, Sass rode right next to Rigby, and smashed him into a current this time.

No, he thought. This was especially dangerous.

The current tugged him right as Rigby tried to tug left, for no use. It was leading him to places unknown.

Then he remembered a technique in his book *Aquatic for Newbs*. He had to spin three hundred sixty degrees in the direction he wanted to go. He memorized a lingo for it. Grab, twirl, jab.

He had to first grab his hands really tight on the stick. Then, he'd shift his weight towards the left, to get out with a twirl that might be made multiple times. And lastly, he'd have to jab his leg on the subracer in an outward direction to slow. This was called a spinner. The only downside: Only professional Aquatic racers had done this before.

"Grab, twirl, jab. Grab, twirl, jab…" he said. "Here I go."

He grasped his hands tightly on the stick, and twirled. He twirled with amazing speed. One, two, three, *four* twirls until he got out of the current. Most can only do three!

Finally, he jabbed right out of the current and braked. He came to an abrupt stop. As happy as he was, he needed to win.

He zoomed so fast; most things passed by like a blur. He saw a finish line up ahead. And Sass was closer to it than he was.

Rigby put all he had into his subracer. But it still wasn't enough. He might not win, but he could stop Sass from winning. *This could get dangerous,* Rigby thought.

Aiming for Sass's Morrose, he slammed into it with utmost speed, right before the finish line. Technically, there were no fouls, but you could get eliminated for non-sportsmanship like conduct. That could set you back a place.

He saw that Sass's subracer had a large dent in it, and it seemed as if she had troubles getting the engine going. She was behind the finish line.

Rigby checked where he was. He was in front of it. He had won!

He got off his Swifthaste, but he wasn't welcomed a victory. Coach Sirump was angry.

"That's non-sportsmanship like conduct!" the Coach yelled. He ran over to Rigby, really angry. But when he came up closer, he smiled. "Good job," he whispered. "I will call that even. I installed a camera on your subracer, and saw that Sassina hit you into a current. Nice spinner," and left to reprimand Sass.

Rigby was left astonished as he got off the subracer. *He won.*

Everyone got out of their suits, including Frank Mason. He had to navigate the Creepy Current on his own after the whale fart exploded his trackcode.

"One last announcement for you all," Coach Sirump said, after they had all gathered by the lake to finish up for the day. "I'd like to announce our winner for today."

Sass scowled.

"Rigby Cross!"

Random people, and even a few people he knew crowded around him and whooped with joy. Rigby thought they started getting handsy, but then he realized they were trying to pick him up on their shoulders.

"Rigby, Rigby, Rigby!" They shouted. Rigby couldn't help but smile. He'd have to tell Francis what happened at dinner.

But he didn't need to. At dinner, Frank and a few of his friends challenged Rigby to see how many jalapenos they could have before they had to stop themselves. Frank easily won, since he used to grow up on a farm that grew jalapenos. It was mostly what he'd eat all the time, so he was used to it. They also congratulated Rigby on winning, and on successfully channeling a whale toot.

After dinner, he went to bed quickly.

10
Guiding the Holy Spirit

Rigby woke up the next day very tired. He couldn't sleep in from winning the race yesterday, which was unfortunate. He got out of bed and quickly dressed into his uniform.

"Francis?" Rigby asked. He couldn't find him, so he must be already in the Entrance Room eating breakfast.

He exited the motel and entered HEB.

He noticed Barb again and nodded *'Sup*. Barb did the same.

Rigby got his favorite meal, a bacon and egg burrito, and sat down where he saw Francis looking at the schedule on the wall.

"Rigby!" he said as Rigby came over to him.

"What?" Rigby asked.

"You're not going to have math or Bible studies today! Lucky! Well, I actually like Bible studies, but whatever."

Rigby didn't understand Francis so he looked at the schedule himself. Shocked, he found out he had Spiritual Defense all day today.

"Nice," Rigby said, grinning.

After breakfast, he took the stairs to the Spiritual Defense Room.

"Welcome, Mr. Cross." Mr. Gravelbard said.

"Hello," Rigby said back.

All the students arrived already. Rigby must've been late, so he took a seat.

"Today, class, we are going to do something different for a change," Mr. Gravelbard said.

Someone next to Rigby smiled. "I like change."

"We are going to go to the Spiritual Guidance Room to learn about the gifts of the Holy Spirit and harness them for defense."

Everyone groaned, regretting the change.

"Spiritual Guidance!" Frank groaned.

"Yup," Mr. Gravelbard said. "Follow me."

He walked out of the classroom, followed by Rigby and the rest of the class.

Rigby caught up to Frank. "What do you learn in Spiritual Guidance?"

Frank sighed. "Everything you learn in Spiritual Defense, except without weapons and more thought instead of do."

Rigby frowned. That was boring.

They entered the Spiritual Guidance classroom, and the first thing Rigby saw was McKinzie Hallow. She gave him the evil eye and scowled.

Rigby tried to hide behind Frank.

"Hello, Amy," Mr. Gravelbard said to Ms. Abble.

"Hello, Tomé. Welcome. Are we going over the gifts of the Holy Spirit?"

He nodded. "My students will stand up behind the classroom, if you don't mind."

"Okay, sounds good." she responded.

All the Spiritual Defense students groaned.

"Now we have to *stand*!" A few people said.

"My legs might go out!"

Rigby had the feeling they were just complaining to pass the time.

"Alright, students," Ms. Abble said. "There are seven gifts of the Holy Spirit. Sassina, can you name them?"

Sass wasn't listening; she was asleep.

Ms. Abble grunted. "Okay, what about Claudia?"

"They are knowledge, wisdom, counsel, piety, fear of the Lord, strength, and fortidude."

A few laughs erupted from the Spiritual Defense students. "It's *fortitude*," Frank laughed. "What do forts and dudes have to do with the Holy Spirit?!"

Claudia grimaced. "Maybe Jesus might send the Holy Spirit to dudes who live in forts!" she snapped. "Maybe they—"

"All right, be quiet," Ms. Abble commanded.

"Yes, Claudia. You are correct. Knowledge, wisdom, counsel, fear of the Lord, piety, and *fortitude* are the seven gifts. Originally in the Hebrew Bible, there were only six. But fear of the Lord was mentioned twice. In the Latin Vulgate translation, one of the fear of the Lord were translated into piety. What does piety mean? McKinzie?"

"It means faithfulness to God," she said.

"Good job." Ms. Abble responded. "Knowledge and wisdom are very similar, if not the same. Fortitude and strength are similar too. Piety, as McKinzie explained, is faithfulness to God, while fear of the Lord is along the same lines. Similarly, there are only about four gifts of the Holy Spirit that are similar. But however, they are slightly different."

Frank Mason raised his hand.

"Yes," Ms. Abble said.

"So, what it seems like you're saying, is that there are only four gifts of the Holy Spirit, not seven," he said.

"No, but you're on the right track. There are seven gifts of the Holy Spirit, but four are very similar, if not, the same. Today, we will be using four gifts to harness and practice to ward off sin," she said.

Frank hid a scowl behind Thomas. "See what I mean," he said to Rigby. "I don't even understand what she's saying. Spiritual Guidance is kind of boring."

Rigby raised his hand. "What are the four gifts we're practicing?"

Ms. Abble smiled. "Yes, thank you Rigby. We will be working on knowledge, strength, counsel, and piety. I will pair all of you up."

Ms. Abble and Mr. Gravelbard starting grumbling and pairing their students up. It was always a student from Spiritual Defense paired up with a student from Spiritual Guidance.

Rigby was unfortunately paired up with McKinzie Hallow. He was just glad he wasn't paired up with Sass.

They walked outside in their assigned pairs, and stood thirty feet apart from each other.

"The first gifts we will practice on is knowledge and counsel. These ones will be easy, which I will just instruct you on. You must read the Bible often and practice the good acts done in it," Ms. Abble said.

"As for piety, whenever you are about to do something wrong, know how it hurts God. Not only that, but you can get punished. Fear that he can do anything he wanted with you. He is ever merciful, but remember, if you sin too much, you gnaw the cord bonding you and the Lord together. Only acts of good will tape and fix the cord. Repentance and receiving the sacraments you can will be the best help also."

Rigby thought this was good information. Sure, it was boring, but it was nice to know there were ways to avoid sin.

"Now, for strength. This gift can be very generic and vague. So, we will narrow it down to one." Ms. Abble said. "This is where you come in, Tomé."

Mr. Gravelbard cleared his throat. "Strength can be a physical advantage—"

Cheers and happy voices erupted from the boys. "—or mentality can be strength."

Most guys sighed. "You can't go to the gym for that," Frank sighed.

"Unless the gym is flashcards or trial and error," Thomas spoke quietly.

Frank shook his head and smiled. "Told you this guy was smart," he said to Rigby.

Rigby smirked under Mr. Gravelbard's teaching.

"Today we will be practicing how to combine physical and mental strength," Mr. Gravelbard continued. Here are some steps. One, stand straight and tall, but don't put too much effort into doing so, because you will exhaust yourself to quite an extent with the following. Two, look your partner in the eyes."

McKinzie looked at Rigby's.

Rigby made funny faces at her for an attempt to break eye contact. It didn't work, unfortunately.

"On the next step, imagine what you want to do to that person." Then he quickly added, "But don't do anything harmful, make it good rather than bad."

Too late for Frank. His partner, Claudia Jubilee, suddenly disappeared in a cloud of mist.

A few people laughed, but most looked scared. Of all people, Ms. Abble was most mad. Claudia was her favorite student.

She expanded her hands and a ball of light appeared. She threw it at the spot where Claudia was and she appeared.

Gasps and murmurs ensued from the students. "Are you okay, Claudia?" Ms. Abble asked. Claudia nodded but looked pale. "I—I saw a white palace," she said.

Everyone gasped once more and looked at Frank.

Frank paled. "I didn't try to kill her!" he explained. "I just needed a break from her for a couple of seconds!"

When the teachers weren't looking, she stuck her tongue out at him. Frank returned it, but Ms. Abble caught him just as he did so.

"Frank Mason! Go to the corner on the side of the building! Immediately!"

He put his hands up and surrendered toward the corner. But this happening would soon make people like Frank even more.

Everyone tried to do things to their partner. Some tried to copy Frank, but apparently nobody wanted to rid their partner bad enough because it didn't work.

McKinzie kept grunting and clenching her fists, making Rigby want to laugh, but he held it in not to be rude. Suddenly, something very peculiar happened.

Rigby felt bigger, stronger, and–magical? He looked down at his hands, which weren't hands anymore. They were *hooves*. He looked at the rest of his body and found that he was a bright, white horse.

McKinzie made a mocking smile at him.

People started laughing at him and suddenly Rigby became weary that his guess might've been wrong. He somehow plucked a piece of hair from his head with his hooves, or *neck* in this case, and found that it was silver. *Can horses have silver manes?* He asked himself. *Am I even a horse? Hmmm, I'm hungry now. But I feel like I want to eat grass.* To his dismay, he wasn't a horse. He was something much worse.

"He's a unicorn!" Claudia shouted. More giggles occurred.

Sure enough, Rigby felt his head and a pointy thing on his head. He whinnied and stomped his new hooves.

"All right, all right, enough laughing," Ms. Abble said, though Rigby had a feeling that she was saying this against her personal desire.

McKinzie Hallow flashed one more mocking smile at Rigby and he was at once turned back into himself. He wished he stopped having a desire to munch on grass though.

Since he was mad, he had to get back at McKinzie. He wouldn't pull a Frank, so he made sure to make fun of McKinzie right back.

He thought of something embarrassing. He'd always hate it when his fellow classmates back at St. Anne's would talk about his picture that showed what Google predicted he'd look like in a hundred years. It was obvious Rigby looked the oldest and frail, and he knew it was true, but never admitted it.

Now, McKinzie would pay for turning him into a unicorn.

He imagined his least favorite elder he knew, named Mrs. Nettlesome. She'd always snap at Rigby every time she saw him looking at a screen. She'd say, "Get off ye ol' buttocks and play like a regular man!" Then if Rigby was close enough, she'd whack her cane at him.

It was annoying. At his birthday parties, his mom would always invite a few elderly people from where she worked, and they were in fact very nice. It was just Mrs. Nettlesome that was very, nettlesome.

Rigby pictured an image of Mrs. Nettlesome where McKinzie was. He added a few words she'd say too. Now he understood why McKinzie had a hard time doing so. He had to imagine every single detail of purple clothing, small stature, white hair color, and even a brown cane.

After a minute of uninterrupted thinking, McKinzie changed into Mrs. Nettlesome with a pop.

Now everyone started laughing. "He got her right back!" Frank hollered.

"Get off ye ol' buttocks ye young whippersnapper!" McKinzie/Mrs. Nettlesome yelled. Then her face quickly acted confused, but Rigby made her look mean again.

Now Rigby flashed a mocking smile at McKinzie. "That was good," Mr. Gravelbard said. "Now turn her back into herself."

Rigby sighed. "Fine." Even a few of his classmates pouted.

So, that just about ended class for Rigby and the rest of the students.

Rigby made sure to go to bed early later and maybe crack a few jokes about McKinzie at dinner.

11
Pappy's Future

Weeks and weeks into school, Rigby's grades started to slip. He didn't know if his late-night lessons with Mr. Highten were lowering them or because he wanted to focus on Aquatic more.

The lessons with Mr. Highten bothered him. Rigby asked Mr. Highten what the grandfather clock in his office was for.

He responded, "Nothing important. Merely for decoration. Remember, let's stick to the subject: How to rationally decide if bravery is the best option." That was the farthest he could go for knowledge.

Even though Mr. Highten told Rigby not to tell anyone about the letter, he told Francis.

"Wow, that's cool!" Francis said at lunch one day. "Wonder what you'll learn about!"

After that talk, Rigby's grades started climbing up once more. He started getting 80% and 90%. Though not as good as Francis's. Francis had something like 101%.

He was getting average, which was okay for Rigby. He even started writing down some of his

The Epic of Rigby Cross

dreams, about once or twice a week; all of his dreams had corn for eyeballs.

If that wasn't creepy enough, they'd sometimes turn to popcorn.

His Aquatic skills were much better now; he could finally go through some of the three obstacle courses, though it took him one full hour instead of thirty minutes.

The one of the hardest obstacle courses was the Ink Cloud. It was literally a pitch-black spot of ink in the lake that was about two miles.

The Kelp Crossroads were simple, since it was just random kelp growing. Rigby swore some of it tried to grab his subracer and condense it. The Rugged Rocks were only a little easier, because you had to constantly swerve to avoid cracks and crevices made of rocks. Rigby didn't ever dare take short cuts, because everyone seemed scared at what happened to Greggory Unfort.

Spiritual Defense was his best grade. He learned some basic sword fighting, and defeated an enormous, overweight, flying cat that spit fire. It was called a feliferno. He also slayed a canis stupidus, which was a miniature chihuahua looking dog on steroids with psychosis and hydrophobia. Talk about the foam afterwards.

His favorite sword had a blade made of ruby. Whenever he made a cut with it, the sword would leave a sting like fire. It made evil creatures back off.

The emerald was okay, but it only paused the blood flow in the attacked creature for a few seconds, which only confused the animal. If you were lucky, it caused a minor, temporary blood clot.

Not only did he learn to summon things from the intermediate Realm between Heaven and Earth, but he also learned how to put things in it. It was quite easy.

All you had to do was lay your hand up, and imagine what you wanted put in the Realm. The only downside was that the object had to be stored by *you* and you had to imagine the object precisely.

There was a kind of platform where you could store things in a spot in the Realm where everyone could get it, but somebody could easily steal it.

A month before the school closed for break, Francis finally found a lead on the mysterious clock.

"It's called the Cursed Time-Teller. Most who are familiar with it, though most aren't, call it Pappy's Future."

Rigby blinked. "Pappy's Future. Okay." He said laughing. "Where'd you find out about this?"

"In the library."

Rigby obviously was really bad at looking.

"It looks exactly as you described it," Francis continued, "all curved at the top, and boxy at the bottom, coated in an antique rustic brown. Supposedly, the holder can change the past, present, and future. The people who cursed it lived in the seventeenth century, under the names of Ronald Marter and Figaro Inventeur. Both died protecting it from pirates. Ronald Marter went rogue after losing his way on a trip to the Outyard."

It seemed crazy, but Ronald Marter could have been the psychotic spirit that killed one of the apprentices last year like Frank mentioned. The spirit did yell about a clock...

"That's all I could find. Ms. Emaciat looked suspicious to me. She seemed to be getting on to figuring it out."

Rigby nodded.

"So, like, if I wanted all the time in the world, I just hold it and ta-da?"

Francis frowned. "Not like that, I think. It seems like you actually have to want something really bad."

Rigby then knew this was what the dragon in his dream wanted. The clock could essentially do whatever it wanted, as long as the dragon tried. Rigby had to protect Mr. Highten's clock.

"I know this is off subject, but did you return the Iserd yet?" asked Rigby.

99

Francis nodded. "Yeah, but McKinzie Hallow almost caught me. I put it in her desk drawer in the Motel."

Rigby whistled. "And she didn't see you at all?!"

Francis looked impatient. "No! I told you, she almost caught me. She walked past her room just as I hid in the closet. Once she passed the room, I put it in a slip of her drawer and left at top speed."

Rigby was amazed.

During Mr. Highten's lesson, Rigby asked, "What do you know about the Cursed Time-Teller?"

Mr. Highten flinched. "About what?"

Rigby pointed to the grandfather clock beside his chair. "That."

Mr. Highten sighed. "I suppose it was about time you figured it out. Did Francis help you?"

"No." Rigby lied. Mr. Highten nodded.

"I would not like to tell you more than you already know. Information is a powerful thing."

"Well, I know enough." Rigby said with a matter of fact.

Mr. Highten raised his eyebrows.

Then Rigby said, "The Cursed Time-Teller, or Pappy's Future, can basically change time for you, as long as you want it bad enough. I figured the dragon in my dream is after it, but it might harm him also. I think we need to protect it."

Mr. Highten pondered that. "I think this is none of your concern, but I appreciate your offer.

Rigby knew this was coming. He consented, but he would protect it in time when he could figure out how to.

Then the ground shook. The building rumbled, and Mr. Highten and Rigby froze. The room shook again, this time dust from the ceiling fell.

"Get to the Motel, now. Tell this to everyone you pass. We are under attack. Your dream, I believe, warned you." Mr. Highten said sternly. Then he added, "All Spiritual Defense students will fight along with the teachers. NOW!"

Rigby did as he was told and left the room.

He bolted to the Entrance Room, fear pounding in his chest. *What was going on?*

"Everyone!" he said, as scared eyes looked at him. "Everyone needs to go to the Motel. NOW!"

Many did without a word.

Rigby turned left and then straight into the Chemistry Laboratory.

It was exactly like the Spiritual Defense room, except it had vials of glowing, flammable, and toxic substances that changed color under microscopes.

"To the Motel!" he shouted. "We're under attack!"

Francis and Matthew were in there. They ran up to him. "What's going on!?" Francis asked.

"HEB's being attacked! Hurry! Tell the Craftsmanship class right now! HURRY!" Francis and Matthew bolted.

Rigby ran toward the Spiritual Defense classroom. "We need Defense! We're being attacked! Mr. Gravelbard! We need to assemble an army consisted of teachers and students!"

The ground rumbled as a piece of the roof collapsed. Mr. Gravelbard nodded gravely and set off as fast as his body would carry him.

Students lined up in a complicated formation, grabbed bows, arrows, and swords, and went out to the battle raging below. Rigby grabbed a light, ruby sword from the teacher's desk and went downstairs to the grounds.

Massive dragons like the ones Rigby saw in his dream were breathing fire and destroying all they could in sight. Doves were in the air too, fighting the dragons, but did very little damage.

Most students were at the Motel, but many were fighting. It was a major disadvantage fighting on the ground, while fending off dragons from above.

All the graduals were using techniques in *Dragon Slayer* on the dragons. The moves were great, and about three students fought a single beast at a time with swords. They slayed one, but were exhausted and one had his left side of his face partially burned.

Unfortunately, there were about ten dragons in all.

Rigby knew nothing of this yet. All he studied was theory. He'd learn more when he was a learner.

Skilled learner archers shot arrows at dragons from the sky, only injuring them though. Rigby saw flaming arrows, which set fire to whatever it hit. They always hit the dragons, but the beasts seemed to be immune to fire.

Ms. Abble stood by the Aquatic Lake. She made hand formations, and cast them out at dragons. A few doves appeared from her hands and flew like a kamikaze pilot toward the dragons. Unfortunately, they got charred to a crisp by fire.

She put her hands on her hips with a frown. "That was annoying. I'm good at Spiritual Guidance, I teach it too."

Rigby almost asked if she needed help, but he didn't want to be rude. Ms. Abble saw Claudia Jubilee running from a dragon. Everyone knew this was her favorite student. Her eyes opened wide as she ran toward Claudia. "How dare you malevolent beast scare my student!"

She pulled her hand back, and motioned it violently at the dragon. Blinding yellow light shot out of her hand and exploded the dragon to pieces.

Ms. Abble gasped and victory-kicked the air. "Booyah!"

Rigby hid a laugh. It was funny to see a teacher so excited.

Rigby saw Matthew about to get charred by a dragon, so he launched his sword as far and fast as he could at the dragon. It definitely saved Matthew, because it hit the dragon's eye and sat under a fallen stone tower. It roared in frustration. Matthew smiled weakly and waved at Rigby. "GET TO THE MOTEL!" Rigby shouted.

Matthew did so without further ado.

Rigby might've saved Matthew's life, but the dragon didn't care. It charged at Rigby with rage.

12

Barb Aric

Rigby ducked avoiding the dragon's fiery breath. *I need to get my sword,* thought Rigby. He obviously couldn't defeat a dragon without some kind of weapon.

While he prayed Hail Marys in the back of his head, he ducked, rolled, and jumped running toward his sword. He felt exhausted just trying to get a weapon.

He army crawled under a fallen tower, and grabbed his ruby sword as fire skimmed the left side of his blue pants.

On his thirtieth Hail Mary, he rolled behind stone wreckage, letting himself rest a few moments. He was safe… but the dragon simply lifted the stone up.

He slid under the dragon, jabbing his sword into its belly, hearing an angry roar of agony from the dragon. Blood poured from its stomach, staining the grass below it, from a charred brownish yellowish color to red.

Rigby miraculously jumped over a huge breath of fire and climbed up the leg of the dragon. The skin felt like fire, and Rigby quickly jumped off. He sliced his sword at the dragon, injuring its leg. The dragon roared, and Rigby knew the dragon was losing blood and advantages too fast to win.

Its wings flapped rapidly because Rigby put a few dents in it, slowing it down. It flew away lopsided without a steady wing beat or leg movements until it hit the ground and never stirred again.

Rigby breathed a sigh of relief, except it got interrupted from a scream. He whipped his head in its direction. McKinzie Hallow was in a tower surrounded by a dragon flying over, who was teasing her with fire.

Oh great, Rigby thought. *The damsel in distress needs saving from a dragon while trapped in a tower.* Then he added this with much sarcasm. "Great. I could seriously use a fairy tale to be in," and "How did she even get up there in the first place?"

Frank looked at Rigby and used facial signals to ask if he would help McKinzie. Rigby nodded, and ran toward the tower with his sword sheathed. He climbed very slowly, with a group of apprentices that just arrived from a field trip. They held back defending Rigby as he climbed the tower. *Don't look down, don't look down.*

At last, with many efforts and heaving, Rigby got to the top. He signaled the apprentices away with a thumbs up. He quickly found McKinzie Hallow, because she was emitting ear splitting screams at the top of her lungs.

"SHUT UP!" Rigby shouted, which got her attention.

"Oh, Rigby! The d–dragon!"

Rigby rolled his eyes and said, "Yeah, I heard. I think I might've gone deaf."

McKinzie nodded sheepishly. "I'm sorry about the unicorn."

"Your fine. We're even now that you turned into a grandma. Listen, are you afraid of heights?"

They ducked under a breath of fire.

"I am now since this experience!" she said.

"You have to do it, jump! Ms. Abble is right there to slow your fall!"

"B–but I can't!" she stammered.

Rigby scowled. *If I have to be in a fairy tale situation, at least make the princess do it.* "Well, stay here while I fight the dragon, okay?!"

She nodded.

There was a door in the tower, so she hid in it. Fatefully, the trapdoor was broken, and didn't work. She had to stay in the tower. Rigby had a phobia of trapdoors since what happened at the Bank of Christ.

The dragon circled around him. It came very close to him and Rigby jumped.

Its skin made Rigby's clothes heat up, so he quickly attacked the dragon with his sword as swiftly as possible.

It roared and wailed. Rigby jumped back on to the tower, feeling dizzy. He noticed his uniform was nothing but shreds. He was glad underwear was invented. Also, he was *not* wearing his lucky undies today.

The dragon almost knocked the tower down trying to steady itself. Just when it was going to knock the tower down, it transformed into *Barb*.

Rigby was baffled. "Barb?" Barb was in torn clothes too, except his undies weren't on display. Barb smiled with evil glee in his eyes. "So, we meet again."

13
The End of the Beginning

There was no way in this world that Rigby though Barb would be a dragon.

"Barb," Rigby said through gritted teeth.

He smiled. "I bet you're glad to see me?" he asked sarcastically.

Rigby snarled. "It was you."

"Yes. It was I who planned the attack, Cross. I, who was never there. I, who infiltrated the powers of your leader. I made everyone believe that I had existed."

Rigby stood in a poised position, ready to fight.

"Of course, you had to get in the way." He emphasized "you" with much abhorrence.

"*You* were immune to my infiltrations. *You* who continually stopped my attempt from stealing your soul."

"Wait. *You* tried to kill me once before?!"

Barb smiled.

"At the bank." Rigby said. "You tried to send me to the abyss and kill me, though you took a form of a woman."

Barb laughed maliciously. "Partially, Cross. I didn't try to *kill* you at first. Your Master has power over the dead. Mine has much power over the living. Or at least, it is growing. We needed you alive, so we could cloud your mind with thoughts to work for my master. You would make a great warrior with my Master's team. Now step aside and let me have the clock."

Rigby only pondered this for half a second. "Ha! Never, Barb. And I'll live in a fiery hovel?! Never will I ever, you demon!" Rigby shouted.

Barb sighed. "Well, it was worth a try. You'll just have to die, for sure, this time." Barb charged. Rigby and Barb met sword with sword. Where Barb's sword came from, Rigby didn't know. But he didn't care.

CLINKSH! Rigby aimed a hit for the neck of Barb, but he deflected it. He went down low, to be deflected once more. They were neck and neck many times, but none managed to kill the other. Barb managed to trim Rigby's hair, but that was about the most progress any of them made.

Just as Rigby thought Barb was about to lose, Barb cut some skin on Rigby's arm. "Ah!" he yelped.

Barb then stuck his hand out toward Rigby.

Immediately, Rigby felt a lot of pain. He fell to the ground, clutching his sword to try to lessen it.

Dragons appeared and headed straight for Rigby. *This is it,* Rigby thought, feeling defenseless.

Barb headed for another tower.

Barb's probably going to get Pappy's Future.

But then a bright, yellow aura of light appeared right next to him. He looked over and saw an angel. Rigby wanted to cower down in awe, but he remembered from the Bible that angels extremely disliked people bowing down at them instead of God. Also, he was cowering in lessening pain. The angel nodded at Rigby, and Rigby nodded back.

He got up, and they charged at the oncoming dragons, together.

*   *   *

He landed on the roof at the tower Barb entered. He thanked the angel, and it flew away toward the sky. *Where's Barb?* He thought.

He went down the steps into the Spiritual Defense room. Barb wasn't there. He visited the chem lab; not there.

But then Rigby had an idea. "I'm such a dummy," he muttered. Pappy's Future was obviously in Mr. Highten's office!

Rigby sprinted down the stairs and into Mr. Highten's office.

Barb was already touching the clock. He smirked at Rigby. "Bring me to my Future," he said. Light began to shine from it.

"No!" Rigby shouted. He couldn't afford to lose his future to Barb Aric. He threw his sword as his last hope, aiming for Pappy's Future.

Light began to shine all around him. His sword had to destroy the clock!

Now all Rigby could see was light which was blinding his eyes.

Then, he heard a crash. An explosion knocked him off his feet and he flew over the tower toward his death.

*　　　　*　　　　*

Rigby didn't remember much, except for the fact that he was extremely exhausted. So exhausted, in fact, that he couldn't sit up. Literally.

He opened his eyes, and found himself in an outdoor hospital. It looked like one of those Red Cross tents. Actually, instead of a red cross, it was a brown cross that resembled the one Jesus died on.

"He's awake!" came a voice. Francis, Matthew, McKinzie Hallow, and Mr. Highten came over. Matthew looked fine, Francis had a black eye,

McKinzie looked unhurt, and Mr. Highten was severely mentally damaged.

Rigby smiled weakly in a small bed, with his head propped up on a fluffy pillow. *I am alive.*

"Greetings?" he said. Everyone was laughing, with tears coming out of their eyes.

"You're alive!" exclaimed Francis.

"Uh, yeah. I mean, yay, I'm alive." Rigby tried through aching pains in his legs. Nobody laughed this time, but Rigby didn't care.

"Thank you, Rigby," Matthew said, "for saving my life." Rigby nodded.

Francis said he was happy and whatnot, but they had to leave to help with other matters.

"Rigby," McKinzie Hallow said, "how can I thank you?" she was on the verge of tears.

Rigby frowned, thinking. "Donuts?" Rigby spoke.

She laughed.

"Okay, maybe I can buy you some later." Then she added, "But seriously, what do I need to repay you for?"

Rigby didn't know what to say. Honestly, he could really go for some hot, fried chocolate bars, but it seemed like McKinzie wanted to feel like she sincerely paid off a debt. But he had an idea.

"Um, you can forgive me and Francis for not having manly manners and for stealing your Iserd?"

She nodded. "Wait," she said, "you stole my Iserd?" Rigby nodded. She made a weird face at him, like looking at him if the public would still call him handsome if he wore a unicorn costume.

"Forgiven." She agreed simply.

"Thanks," Rigby said, feeling a lot of weight fall off his shoulders he didn't knew he had.

She paused for a really long time, like she wanted to say something, but didn't know how to. But suddenly in a rush, she swooped down and gave him a peck on the cheek. "Thank you," she said, and left.

Rigby raised his eyebrows. He was like that for a long time, until Mr. Highten cleared his throat.

Rigby snapped back to reality. "Sorry, Mr. Highten."

He chuckled. "No worries, Rigby. The graduals are much more of a concern than that."

Rigby sighed with relief.

"Believe me, I might need a glue remover or something. Maybe someone can make that who's taking Craftsmanship." Mr. Highten pondered that for a moment.

"Anyways, Rigby. This next talk is very important. As you know, Barb and his army, or his Master, will strike once more."

Rigby didn't know that. "What happened to Barb? Did he get the Cursed Time-Teller?"

"No. You tossed your sword at the clock just in time, causing it to explode and send Barb flying off the tower. The students believe he's dead, but I know you know better. His body and soul are in the fire below us. Now more towers require maintenance."

Rigby shivered. "Who was that angel on the tower?"

Mr. Highten frowned. "What angel?"

Rigby smiled, because he knew if nobody else could see the angel, this angel was his Guardian. He was lucky just as he was to see his angel.

"I need you to find the Archangels, like Michael, Raphael, and Gabriel. They will help defeat Barb's Master. Not only that, but they are a part of the seven angels who are destined to end the world by God's command." Said Mr. Highten. Then he added, "I love Revalation."

Rigby wanted to say, "Yeah, I could tell." But he just nodded. Problems never stopped.

"Where will I find them?"

"That, Rigby, will be for you to decide. You can accomplish that however you want. A successful

American general said similar words." He paused. "Good luck." He nodded. "But in the meantime, Rigby, I hope you enjoy healing the wounded."

Rigby groaned as he tried to get up.

"Not now, not now!" said Mr. Highten. "When you're healed." He turned away, but quickly turned back toward Rigby. "Also, you might what to stalk up on new underwear." He walked away.

Rigby frowned, and carefully felt legs. "Seriously?!"

Even after losing half a pair of fabulous underwear, his new assignment seemed distant.

At least it isn't my lucky undies.

Epilogue

Rigby, McKinzie, and Francis sat by the shore of the Aquatic Lake.

Rigby breathed a sigh at the descending sun behind Hadash Eden's church.

Francis looked at him mournfully. "I know," he said.

Rigby looked at the church again. He had just figured out last week that the church had an invisible force field around itself. More dragons had attempted to destroy it, but it seemed to be that God's house didn't want to crumble.

It's forcefield was definitely losing power, but Hadash Eden's Holy Orders wouldn't allow the citizens to give up hope.

Life would be hard for Rigby from now on. He, along with Francis and McKinzie, would set off tomorrow to go into hiding. To where? He didn't even know.

He'd miss his parents and friends. And everyone else he knew. How long would it be until he'd be able to see them again? That was beyond his current knowledge.

Barb Aric and the Accuser were getting too powerful, and Rigby Cross was their main target.

Since he wouldn't let them win, he would have to figure out a plan to stop them while in hiding. He wouldn't know how long to stay hidden. Days, months, maybe even years? Only time would tell.

Even if he figured out how to, he couldn't accomplish it just learning theoretically. He'd just have to *start*.

Mr. Highten had instructed Rigby to search for the archangels, because they might help him defeat the Accuser. Saint Michael had defeated him before, so it was only a matter of time to imprison him again. He also thought it was best to wait to tell Francis and McKinzie about the archangels until he strategized a plan.

But why now? Why couldn't it be later in the future?

Rigby had been reading Revelation when he came across something scary. The Accuser was released every one thousand years. The time before the last he was released was probably about when Jesus died. He might've been released sooner. Add another two thousand years, he would be released in about A.D. 2033. Time was of the essence if Rigby failed. And he had a feeling that the world, including Hadash Eden, would require much sacrifice far beyond their humane ability, for an attempt to win.

There were scarce tools and time; all they had left was luck and hope.

To be Continued...

The Next Part in Rigby's Epic is Here!

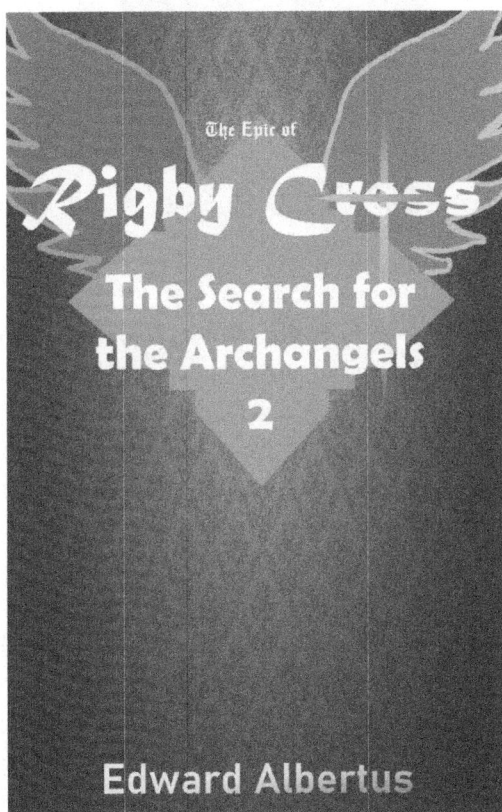

The Epic of

Rigby Cross

The Search for the Archangels

2

Edward Albertus

Coming Soon to Paperback!

About the Author

Edward Albertus is the author of the Rigby Cross series which tells of an arrogant tween boy, who, by inadvertently discovering a new world through a spice shop, becomes humbled from competition, magic, and war. He must learn survival tactics and battle techniques by using the mighty powers mentioned in the Bible before his arch-nemesis Barb Aric destroys the world.

He plans to continue writing fictional stories and hopes more readers can continue reading his books. When he isn't writing, he's publishing reggae music, creating card games, reading, studying, golfing, or hanging out with his dog—an Australian Shepherd named Peter.

To reach out to him, email him at albertusauthor@gmail.com for questions, comments, or concerns. If you would like to support him, feel free to purchase his books and give 5-star reviews!

Want to Know *Your* Opt?

Read the following pages and answer the questions
in your vision to identify your Opt!

You stand in front of the passageway between the airport and the plane you are boarding. For Christmas, your family is taking a trip to Hawaii where you'll enjoy the warmth instead of the cold.

There are many people trying to board and there's word going around that there were more tickets sold than there were available seats, so many people are trying to get in first.

As soon as the airport employees let your family through, people from behind push you and your family in all different directions. Luckily, your little sister grabs your hand just in the nick of time before a larger family of five decides to ram over other kids in order to board.

Clutching your six-year-old sister's hand, you try to move forward and get in front of the others where you began. You are successful and pick up your sister so that your can run faster to find your parents.

You begin to slow down as you approach the plane, but nearing footsteps echo loudly and seem to be coming your way. You don't know what to do. Should you chance it and run on the plane where flight attendants might kick you off and let the other person pass through first, lessening your chances of being able to have a seat on the plane? Or stand firm and turn around to shield your sister from potentially getting knocked down again?

1a. Keep running.

1b. Let the person pass through

1c. Protect your sister and prepare to face what you must.

If you chose **1a**, read this paragraph. You decide to keep running. Your hands are getting tired of holding your sister who weighs at least thirty pounds and you might drop her. So, you set her down and tell her to run with you. Since your sister is much younger than you, she can't quite run as fast and you eventually pick her up because the footsteps are getting louder. When you approach the plane, suddenly they stop. You turn around behind you and see the pilot, who arrived late. "C'mon," she said. "I don't have all day. There are seats for everyone." You breathe a sigh of relief that it wasn't anything bad, and that there are seats for all who boarded. You thank her and try to find your parents. Flip to page 125.

If you chose **1b**, read this paragraph. Since you think it is best to let the person pass through, you stop and wait for them to come. To your surprise, it is just the pilot running late. C'mon," she said. "I don't have all day. There are seats for everyone." You breathe a sigh of relief that it wasn't anything bad, and that there are seats for all who boarded. You thank her and try to find your parents. Flip to page 125.

If you chose **1c**, read this paragraph. You decide to stand in front of your sister, protecting her from what could be someone dangerous. As the footsteps sound louder, a person appears and you find that she's the pilot. "Are you okay?" she asks. "I need to get through or you won't get to Hawaii soon." You blink and apologize for assuming she could've been dangerous. "And don't worry," she adds. "There are seats for everyone. The airport doesn't make mistakes like that." Then you find your parents. Flip to page 125.

As you're looking for your parents down the aisle of the plane, you glance at a man sitting in a seat that you're supposed to sit in according to your ticket.

You see he has sunglasses, jet black hair, and a bright Hawaiian button-up shirt, though no one seems to realizes he exists. As you go closer towards him, you get a really sick feeling. Your stomach begins to hurt and you fear for you and your sister.

As you begin to approach him, at just the right moment, he sticks his foot out and trips you and your sister.

"Hey!" you cry. When you're on the floor, you see a shiny sword on the floor. It has a red blade and a silver hilt.

"Watch where you're going!" he yells.

You look up at him and he tips his sunglasses down to reveal red eyes.

You have never seen anything like this before. He is a threat to you and your younger sister. What do you do?

2a. Grab the sword in an attempt to threaten him, and if need be, use it.

2b. Apologize for you tripping over him, even though he intended to hurt you.

2c. Try to talk to him. Maybe the red eyes you saw were just a trick of the light. Afterall, sometimes people have red eyes in a photo.

If you chose **2a** and grabbed the sword, read this paragraph. Once you grab the sword, you stand up and swing it in front of your sister, blocking his view of her. But the man just smiles, his red eyes glowing even more. "This child has a sword!" he yelped, as if he were suddenly afraid. And just as if people had always noticed him, they heard what he said and began freaking out. Flight attendants and security guards rush over towards you to figure out the commotion. What you are doing is illegal. A child cannot carry a weapon. You try to explain what you've done and your motives, but no one believes you. Especially the part with the red eyes. You, along with your innocent sister, go to jail and miss the trip to Hawaii. (You're opt is now complete. Go to page 130 and check with your opt results)

If you chose **2b**, read this paragraph. "Sorry," you say, nudging the sword under an empty seat behind you so no one could see it. You and your sister stand up. If you were caught holding it, you could get arrested. But the man just smiles, his red eyes glowing even more. You begin to freak out and step in front of your sister, but slowly move away. He cannot accuse you of having a weapon, and you didn't harm him, so he didn't proceed, and left you alone to find you parents and sit in another seat. Flip to page 128.

If you chose **2c**, you are trying to reason with him. You stand up, and though he gets more creepy by the second, you try to keep your cool and reason with him. "Sir, that was awfully rude." You nudge the sword under an empty seat behind you so no one could see it. Afterall, if a kid held a weapon, he'd go to Juvenile Hall most likely. "I'm not really sorry," he said. You hold in your anger. "Well you did. But since you are a human and we all make mistakes, I trust you won't do it again." You leave it at that, and pick up your sister walk back to find another seat by your parents. Flip to page 128.

Once you've found you parents, they give you their seats and go to your original seats where you told them about the man. But strangely, he is not there anymore.

A few hours into the flight, a loud growl erupts from the engine. It happens a few more times and a few people nearby begin to worry.

Sure enough, a scared pilot speaks through the speakers. "We are going down. Our engines have malfunctioned and we will not make it to Hawaii. Pray, beseech, do what you must, for we will not arrive at our destination."

People begin screaming, crying, and yelling in terror. You try to comfort your sister and the people around you, but you yourself are scared and don't know how to pull through. So, what will you do?

3a. Continue calming other people before the plane crashes.

3b. Pray by yourself for everyone.

3c. Try to figure out how to fix the engines.

If you chose **3a**, read this paragraph. You try to keep calming other down, but to no avail. They, just like you deep down inside, know that there is nothing that can be done. (You're opt is now complete. Go to page 131 and check with your opt results.)

If you chose **3b**, read this paragraph. You know that doing anything other than praying wouldn't help the situation. So, you try to clear your mind of the death awaiting you within minutes. It might not save anyone's lives, and it doesn't, but it saved many a soul. (You're opt is now complete. Go to page 131 and check with your opt results.)

If you chose **3c**, read this paragraph. You try to figure out the problem. You cannot find out what the problem is, but you do know how to save people. You tell them to follow safety procedures and put on a lifejacket. You are so busy helping other people and not yourself, so you won't live to see if it worked or not. (You're opt is now complete. Go to page 131 and check with your opt results)

Opt Results!

Your Opt is Now Confirmed!

If you chose... (The most of a single opt is what your result is)

1a. = 1 Diffident
1b. = 1 Munificent and 1 Sagacious
1c. = 1 Valiant and 1 Vigorous

2a. = 1 Valiant and 1 Vigorous
2b. = 1 Sagacious and 1 Munificent
2c. = 1 Diffident

3a. = 1 Munificent
3b. = 1 Diffident and 1 Sagacious
3c. = 1 Valiant and 1 Vigorous

If there's a tie...You tested for an Opt Hybrid. Though very common, your brain is wired for all the opts you tied in. Mr. Highten usually knows which opts to pick even with a tie, so you may choose either one you think you fit best for your final decision.

Sagacious   Valiant   Diffident
Vigorous   Munificent

Made in the USA
Las Vegas, NV
30 December 2023